MONSTERS AFTER DARK

A BEASTLY PARANORMAL ROMANCE ANTHOLOGY

NORA ASH LEANN RYANS MEREL PIERCE
L.V. LANE V.T BONDS LESLIE CHASE
OPHELIA BELL GODIVA GLENN CASS ALEX
ISOELLEN

RETICENT DESIRE PUBLICATIONS

Monsters After Dark:
A Beastly Paranormal Romance Anthology

Cover Art Designed By Coverluv

ISBN: 978-1-7338370-8-8

CONTENTS

THE DEMON'S BARGAIN

BY NORA ASH

THE DEMON'S BARGAIN

NORA ASH

This is what you get when you're desperate enough to take life advice from a guy named Barry. Especially if Barry runs a tattoo-slash-corner store in the bad part of town, and smells like he only showers once a year for black Sabbath.

The ritual, not the band.

I gritted my teeth and glared at the tea-aged page containing the "summoning ritual" Barry swore would save my ass.

Honestly, fuck Barry. And fuck me for having gotten myself into a bad enough situation that I was willing to try goddamn *witchcraft* to get out of it.

"Hear me, hear me. Thrice, I summon thee. A bargain I offer, a bargain I urge. Hear me, hear me. Thrice, I summon thee. Fire and brimstone—" I paused, the ridiculousness of the words making them hard to spit out.

No doubt Barry and his stoner buddies were currently having a great laugh at my expense.

Maybe I should just leave the country? But that route cost money. Money I didn't have—hence my current predicament.

"Fire and brimstone and ash. Hear me, hear me. Thrice I summon thee—Kurt."

Kurt? I snorted and lowered my arms. Right. If I made it through the week with my thumbs still intact, Barry was going to regret the day he was born.

Okay, so he'd caught me with my fingers in the till, and convincing me to summon a demon named *Kurt* was pretty excellent revenge, but for a wild moment, I'd had just a tiny thread of hope. He'd looked so sincere when he handed me that stupid book, told me he knew about desperation, and that he understood most sane people would think him ridiculous for even suggesting it—but he swore up and down that it was real. That I had nothing to lose by trying.

He was right; I'd called him both insane and ridiculous. But in the end, I'd left with a book of "spells," because when I'd brushed my fingertips over the leatherbound tomb, I'd thought I felt the barest whisper of... *something.*

Apparently, that something was nothing more than desperation. *Quelle surprise.*

I dropped said book on the floor and kicked it out of the circle of table salt I'd drawn in preparation for my first and last encounter with goth culture.

Fuck. Fuck, fuck, *fuck*. I was going to die. The men I owed money to would take my digits first, two at a time. Then my kneecaps. Then my life.

I could try to run. I probably would. They'd find me, of course. There was nowhere on the North American continent I'd be able to hide from this—and even if I'd had the money to leave the country, likely nowhere else. Judging by their accents, they were Russian mobsters, or something to that extent. Definitely internationally connected.

Five more days until they came to collect.

I bent to blow out the five black candles I'd placed around my salt circle, then crossed the floor of the single room that held all my earthly possessions and dropped into bed, clothes, makeup, and all. Skincare is for people who'll live past twenty-one.

Tomorrow I'd figure out how to slip out of town on a quarter tank of gas. Right now, sleep was the only thing that was going to give me any relief from the fear gnawing through my veins like acid.

My heart slammed into my throat, jolting me awake as brutally as if someone had punched me in the face.

I sat up with a gasp and tried to blink the sleep

from my eyes, animal instincts on high alert for whatever had ripped me awake.

He was sitting at the foot of my bed, bathed in the dim light spilling in from the streetlamps, and when our eyes connected, he gave me a small smile that made every hair on my body stand on end as pure terror gripped me by the gut.

"I still have a week!" I blurted, scrambling backward on my narrow bed as if an extra couple feet would save me.

Oh, God, no. Please, please no.

"That's not a lot of time, darling," the stranger purred, that dangerous smile never slipping from his sensual lips. "How about we do something about that, hmm?"

I blinked, my heart skipping a beat as I took in the smokey rasp of his voice and the way he fixed me with his black eyes, as if he wanted to... to *devour* me.

I may have found him attractive, under different circumstances. He had jet-black, perfectly tousled hair, high cheekbones, and a soft mouth, and a black leather jacket and white T-shirt clung to what looked to be a well-shaped body. But the whole hitman-lurking-in-my-bedroom thing kinda killed any sexy vibe he otherwise had going.

"No—no, that's quite alright. I'll pay," I squeaked. "But I still have a week. You can leave."

"Leave?" He quirked a dark eyebrow at me. "Now why would I do that? I was invited, after all."

"I-Invited?" I croaked.

"Invited..." He scooted up the side of my bed until he sat next to me. When he let two fingers walk up my duvet to my hand, I shuddered, too afraid to pull away. His touch was scorching, and this close, his cologne sank into my nostrils. Warm and spicy, with just a touch of something dirty. Animalic. Almost... sulfuric? "...Summoned. Potato, po-tahto. You promised a bargain, so here I am, little dove. Ready to give you what your heart desires."

I blinked. He... was not a hitman? He wasn't here for my debt?

Only then did I notice his lack of accent.

Relief numbed my entire nervous system for a brief, exquisite moment. Then realization dawned, followed by rage.

I slapped his hand away and poked him in the chest. Hard. "Kurt, is it? Kurt the *demon,* here to take all my troubles away? You can tell Barry to go fuck himself. I can't believe he'd go this far. Give me that book? Okay, ha ha, very funny. But send some strange creep into my apartment while I'm sleeping? That's too fucking far. *Get out.*"

Something passed behind Kurt's dark eyes, something sinister that made me clutch the sheets.

"I told you, darling—I'm not going anywhere before we've agreed on a bargain, hmm? I've come very far to meet with you. You shouldn't be rude to a man who's come to help."

"Yeah? Traffic bad between Chicago and Hell?" I bit, reaching for my phone on my makeshift nightstand—a rickety old chair that wasn't strong enough to hold a person. "Get out, right now, or I'm calling the police."

He closed his strong, warm fingers around my wrist, firmly enough to make me drop my phone. "I wouldn't, if I were you."

Okay, this was officially no longer a mean prank. I swallowed and did my best to seem uncowed as I glared at him. "If you don't let go in the next two seconds, I'll scream."

Kurt snorted. "You think your deadbeat roommates will come save you from the big, bad boogeyman? Go ahead."

"Help me! Help!" I screamed as loud as I could, my voice piercing the quiet morning and echoing through my room. I kept screaming, over and over and over.

No one came.

Slowly, I quieted, panting with mounting terror as I stared into the stranger's hard eyes. I didn't have the best relationship with my five roommates—we were all too busy scraping by to socialize much—but I was pretty certain we were on *will-save-you-from-madman* terms. Or at the very least, someone should have come to check out why I was screeching at ridiculous o'clock. Brian worked until midnight, and got real pissy if awakened before noon.

Someone should have come.

Ice-cold terror gripped me by the throat. "What did you do to them?"

Kurt tutted and finally released my wrist. I pulled my arm close to my body and curled all the way into the far corner of my bed, gaze locked on him.

"They'll wake up once you and I are done here, darling," he said softly, reaching out to nudge at my chin.

I swallowed hard and steeled myself against the shiver that went down my spine at his touch. "What do you want, then? Sex? Is that the price Barry wants me to pay for trying to steal from him—getting raped?"

The darkhaired man chuffed through his nose and got to his feet. He shoved his hands into his jacket pockets and took a few steps to where I'd drawn the salt circle last night before he turned back around to me, lips slightly pursed.

"There seems to have been some... ah, *misunderstanding*. Did you not read aloud the ritual? Draw the circle? Light cheap candles? ...Summon a demon?" He pushed at the salt with his foot, giving me a sardonic look. "Is this a case of mistaken identities, hmm? Do I have the wrong address? Is the real summoner perhaps the little old lady downstairs?"

I shuddered at the thought of this guy sneaking into Mrs. Mckinnon's bedroom.

"Look, you can drop the act. I get it—this is my fault for playing along with Barry's witchcraft-is-real bullshit. Ha-ha, desperation will make people do the dumbest things. I don't know what you've done to my roommates, but what's the plan here? Scare me? Mission accomplished—I'm scared. You can go back to Barry now. Please."

I didn't manage to kill the quaver in my voice at the end.

Kurt sighed heavily. "Ah, you're one of *those.* I must admit, usually the non-believers who summon me are teenagers too scared to rebel against their parents with drugs, so they play pretend at being witches. Then *poof*, an actual demon appears, and it's a whole ordeal. You're my first adult without a clue. But okay, let's get this over with."

He held up a hand, and *darkness* crept from it in tendrils. Like thick smoke filling the air around him.

I blinked, about to try to rationalize away what I was seeing, when his face sort of... melted off.

"Oh my God!" I croaked, equal parts disgusted and horrified. "What the fuck?!"

He didn't answer—but he really didn't need to, because in place of the terrifying-but-handsome-human now stood a monster.

It was still shaped like a person, but bigger, with dark, red-tinted scales covering its body and black, curled horns atop its head. Where Kurt's irises had been black before, now his sclera were too, stained like ink on bone.

It smiled at me.

I screamed. I screamed until my throat ached and the numb terror freezing me in place finally released its grip on my body. Mindlessly I hurled myself off the bed and threw myself toward the door —but the second my hand touched the doorknob, something dark closed around me and held me tight.

I wheezed a sob of terror, fighting with everything I had to free myself, but no matter how much I strained, I couldn't move.

"Do you believe me now? Or should I devour one of your roommates in front of you to make sure we're on the same page here?"

"N-No. I b-believe you!" I stuttered. "Don't— don't hurt anyone. P-Please!"

"Good." The darkness released me. I slumped against the door, too shaken to mount another escape attempt.

"Then perhaps we can talk business now, hmm? The drive from Cincinnati was a pain." A strong, warm hand grabbed me by the shoulder and forced me to turn around. To face him.

I gasped and squeezed my eyes shut in a childish attempt at not seeing that *thing* again. It was that or wet myself.

Kurt huffed a sigh and shifted his grip from my

shoulder to my chin, shaking my jaw enough to make my teeth clatter. "Come now, I don't have all night."

A demon. I'd summoned a *demon.* My mind kept circling back to that impossible fact, my brain entirely short-circuiting at my attempt at grasping that demons were *real.*

This had to be some fucked-up fever dream.

Slowly, I cracked an eye open.

Kurt was still standing in front of me—way too close, but thankfully he once again looked very much human. Had I just... hallucinated a monster in his place?

As if triggered by my thoughts, the black of Kurt's irises bled into the whites—a small reminder of what lay underneath his pale skin.

Okay. Not a fever dream.

"Don't, please, don't!" I babbled.

Kurt gave me another of those slanted smiles, but his eyes reverted to normal—or at least to their human states, which possibly wasn't *normal* for him. *Christ.*

"Now that we have that settled..." The demon sauntered back to my salt-circle, giving me room to breathe. He nudged a foot at the white grains again. "What did you call me for, darling? Need money? Or do you desire the favor of a young man's heart? Perhaps you want someone dead? This Barry character, mayhap?"

"Money," I whispered. "Just... Just the money."

Kurt appraised my small room and *tsk*ed. "How... unsurprising. But your wish is my command. How much do you need?"

It was only then that the realization that my harebrained plan of summoning a demon to save my ass from the Russian mob... had actually worked.

There was an actual demon in my bedroom... and he was asking me how much money I wanted, like a leather-clad genie. Bless Barry and whatever goth-y acquaintance he'd stolen that book from.

Despite my fear of his true face, my heart gave a thud of pained relief.

"Can I... Can I just say a number, and you'll provide it?" I asked. It sounded too good to be true, but...

"Sure can, darling," Kurt said, his smile widening without warming a single degree.

"Okay. A hundred million, then," I said, expecting him to laugh. "Wait—two hundred million."

He chuffed through his nose, walked to my makeshift bedside table, and snapped his fingers. Smoke puffed around his hand, and a sheet of paper and an old-fashioned pen appeared on the rickety chair.

Magic. Actual magic. Maybe I shouldn't have been surprised, what with having just learned that demons were real, but seeing non-traumatizing proof of this man's *otherness* was mesmerizing.

Kurt grabbed the pen, pricked his finger on the tip of it, and scribbled across the paper in a few places. Then he moved aside and jutted his chin at me. "There you go. All I need is your pretty little signature, and then two hundred million will be yours."

Cautiously, I edged closer. Despite my desperate eagerness for all my worries to be swept away in a pile of cash, the first alarm bells started to chime. I wasn't super keyed into religion and demons, but I *had* watched a few supernatural TV shows over the years. Demons were supposed to be tricksy. Right?

"Are you trying to trick me? We're talking two hundred million American dollars. Not some obscure currency that's barely worth anything?"

Kurt chuckled. "American dollars," he confirmed.

Hmm. "And you aren't going to deliver it in pennies?" I shot him a hesitant look before I bent over the piece of paper. Most of the text was written in black ink, but certain words were filled in with red the color of freshly harvested blood. The penmanship was impeccable.

It read:

I hereby sell my eternal soul to the demon Kurt, for the price of 200,000,000 USD (*two hundred million dollars), to be paid immediately upon exchange of this contract.*

This agreement is binding. I confirm that I will not seek to circumvent or in any way render this contract null and void. By my signature, I am surrendering full and complete ownership of my soul, and I understand that the demon Kurt can claim his payment for services rendered at any time he so chooses.

Signed,

"Bills or wire transfer?" Kurt asked as I blinked at the last sentence. "Whichever is most convenient for you."

"Wait... What does it mean you can claim your payment at any time you choose?" I asked, darting a glance at his face. "Does this mean... *kill* me?"

Kurt shrugged. "Normally I wait for nature to take its course. I hardly ever claim a soul before its time. Mostly it's there to ensure no surprise immortality-loopholes. Nothing to worry your pretty head about."

"Er..." I bit my lip, an unshakable sense of foreboding creeping along my spine as I took in the predatory gleam in his eyes. I'd never given much thought to the concept of my soul—I'd kind of assumed it wasn't a real thing—but I hadn't much believed in demons, either, and if Kurt was willing to trade two hundred *million* dollars for mine... well, it probably wasn't just a way for religious leaders to manipulate their congregations.

"What... What do you use souls for? What will happen to mine, once you claim it?"

He hummed, shoving both hands into the pockets of his leather jacket. "It depends. The pristine ones, I eat. The darker ones, I keep around for servitude. As for yours... well, I guess we'll have to wait and see what kind of life you lead, won't we, darling?"

"Eat?" I croaked. "You *eat* them?"

"Come now, don't look at me like that. Demons need nourishment too. Did you plan to sit on some cloud, playing the harp for all eternity? You don't strike me as the religious type." He gave me another of those wry smiles that pricked the hairs on the back of my neck. "How much worse can it be, if you were expecting to simply... cease to exist anyway, hmm?"

He had a point. I looked back at the contract and the sharply pointed pen. Whatever thoughts I'd made about dying—and there had been a few since I realized I wouldn't be able to pay back what I owed—I'd always assumed my body would just be worm food. The end. What did I care what happened to me after that?

Except... Except I wouldn't just be worm food. I

had a soul. Presumably, those who didn't get eaten by demons went... somewhere else.

Of course, there was every chance I wouldn't end up kicking it with a pristine soul. Then what? Servitude? *Eternal* servitude. I eyed Kurt again. It seemed the better option, but what did I know? I still remembered what he looked like without his human disguise: a creature of hell.

What if signing this contract meant a literal eternity spent in unimaginable torment?

"I..." I chewed on my lip. "Is there not something else you might want instead?"

Kurt raised both eyebrows. "Instead of your soul? No. The only asset you have is your immortal spirit."

I flushed, the bluntness of that insult smarting more than it should, mostly because it was entirely true. I was nothing, and I had nothing of value to give to anyone, let alone anything remotely worth two hundred million dollars.

"What if—what if it was for less? I don't need all that money. I just need twenty thousand. There has to be something else we can trade."

Kurt's face darkened, that sly smirk slipping off his lips. "I am not here to trade collectibles, human. What did you think would happen when you summoned a demon? That it would be like strolling into a bank and having a pleasant chat about taking out a loan?"

Pleasant chat. Clearly demons didn't have much experience with asking a bank for a loan.

"No, I..." What *had* I been expecting during those feverish few moments I'd hoped that Barry wasn't just pranking me?

A miracle. I'd been hoping for a miracle. I stared at Kurt, at his darkly handsome features and the sneer on his soft lips. His human disguise was clearly crafted to draw people in, but no matter how attractive his physicality, every instinct in my body screamed of his true nature—of the monster that lurked just beneath his pale skin.

This demon was no miracle, of that I was certain. But if he left, my life was forfeit.

The criminals I owed money to may not have been demons, but that wouldn't stop them from mutilating my body before they killed me.

"Servitude," I blurted. "I—I can trade servitude."

Kurt cocked his head at me, eyebrows arched in contemplation. "You want to be my slave, darling?"

"Just... for a week, maybe," I hastily interjected. "In exchange for the twenty thousand."

The demon let out a laugh, deep and rumbly and surprisingly genuine. When he looked at me again, there was wicked amusement in his black eyes. "No, sweet thing. I will not be satisfied with a week of service."

"What, then?" I asked, unable to keep the

pleading note from my voice. "What else do you want?"

He gave me a long, calculating look. I suppressed a shudder as every cell in my body lit up with awareness under his predatory stare.

"One night," he finally said. "You will serve me for one night out of every year, until the day you die. Unless, of course, you change your mind along the way and want to re-bargain that shiny little soul of yours."

I hesitated. One night a year. That didn't seem *too* bad. At least not in comparison to having my digits hacked off. But the way he smirked at me when he said *"re-bargain"* made me think there was a pretty good chance he would try to make that night as unpleasant as possible, until I cracked and offered him my soul instead.

But what choice did I have? He was right—I'd summoned a demon. There was going to be a price. No matter what he wanted from me during our time together, I could make it through one night.

"Okay," I whispered. "One night a year."

Kurt's smile turned sharper. "Excellent." He stepped past me, close enough that I felt the heat of his body, and pressed a finger against the contract. The scent of sulfur wafted from him, and the letters on the page rearranged themselves. "There. Sign."

I forced myself to remain calm despite his continued closeness and let my eyes scan the contract. He had changed the wording to reflect our new agreement. And where it had previously specified my soul, it now said body.

My mouth went dry at the implication. "Is this... Are you going to...?"

"Fuck you?" The bluntness of his words heated my cheeks. "Yes."

"Why?" I blurted.

Kurt arched an eyebrow at me.

"I mean—surely you don't need to enslave someone for sex? You look..." I trailed off with a vague hand gesture toward his exceedingly handsome face. So long as he didn't show a girl what lay beneath, Kurt should have had no problems in that department.

The demon chuckled and reached out a hand to nudge my chin. The warmth of his touch and that dark gleam in his eyes made me shiver.

"Sign the contract, darling," was all he said. I read the warning in his voice loud and clear: his patience was wearing thin. And I did not want to know what happened once it ran out.

One night a year until the day I died. But at least this way, my soul wouldn't be enslaved.

Before I could change my mind, I picked up the pen, pricked my fingertip, and scribbled my name on the contract.

Kurt looked at my signature and smiled. "A pleasure doing business with you, *Emma.*" He snapped his fingers, and the paper disappeared in a puff of black smoke.

There was something ominous about the way he'd said my name, as if reading it gave him intimate knowledge of me. Power.

I shuddered. "Now what?"

The demon gave me one of his slanted smiles. "Now you pay your first installment."

"I... Did you...?"

"Uphold my end?" He huffed and snapped his fingers again. Another waft of sulfur hit my nostrils, but I didn't see any magic this time. "Check your account. I'll wait."

Hesitantly, I reached for my phone and logged into my banking app. I drew in a sharp breath at the sight of my balance. Twenty thousand dollars.

When I looked back up from my phone, Kurt was watching me with only a hint of a smirk lingering on his soft lips. The rest of his face was a blank mask, though his eyes... Those black, soulless eyes watched me with *hunger*.

"Are you satisfied?" His last word rumbled with an unmistakable purr.

I didn't answer him. Under different circumstances, I would have been a lot less hesitant about the price I had to pay for my salvation. He really was gorgeous—in his human form. Defined features, soft lips, haunting eyes. Dark, perfectly tousled hair. and a body so strong even his leather jacket couldn't hide the width of his shoulders and chest, nor his tapered waist and powerful thighs.

Something stirred in my abdomen as I let my gaze wander over him, and I flushed hot. Really? Had it really been *that* long, that my starved vagina was this quick to forget what he looked like beneath his skin-suit?

Kurt quirked a knowing smirk at me. Somehow the bastard *knew*.

I forced my blush down and glared at him. "Are you going to tell me why you have to blackmail women to sleep with you, now that I've signed your contract?"

"Darling... I don't have to *blackmail* anyone for sex." He moved then, stalking toward me at a casual pace that didn't match the hunger in his black gaze. "I don't have to barter, trick... coerce." He only stopped when he was right in front of me, so, so close. "I can simply take it. With or without consent."

I swallowed hard at the way his eyes dipped to my lips. There was still a good amount of fear stuck in my system, but the pounding in my blood was no longer entirely from adrenaline. This close, his unnatural body heat leached through my clothes and brushed against my skin, and he smelled like sulfur and man. It shouldn't have been appealing, but that same traitorous something down low softened as I drew in a shaky breath.

"So why didn't you?" I rasped.

"Hmm," he purred. When his hand came up to brush against my cheek, I quivered before I could steel myself. "Would you have liked that, Emma? For a monster to force his way between your thighs? Hold you down? Ravage your body while you pleaded for it to stop?"

"No," I croaked, frustrated that my panties were soaked through even as fear gripped my spine at the picture he painted. "O-Of course not."

"Such pretty lies," he crooned. He slipped his free hand around my waist and pulled me close, leaning in so he could whisper directly into my ear, "I smell you, darling. Your cunt is gushing for me."

"Pig!" I gasped—because if I didn't clutch on to the anger at his crudeness, I knew I would be lost. Swept away on a tide of dark desire. Jesus, how could his mere presence do this to me? Minutes ago, all I'd felt at his nearness was intense fear. It was all I should have been feeling now.

"Hmm," he purred again. When he finally released me, I sagged with relief as some of that intense heat lifted and my mind cleared a little. "Get on the bed."

My relief vanished instantaneously, but I obeyed. This was the bargain I had struck.

"Bare yourself to me," he said when I knelt on my narrow mattress.

My hands shook as I pulled my shirt over my

head, baring my breasts. I'd ditched my bra the second I came home last night.

Kurt growled, making my nipples tighten and a shock of awareness run up the length of my spine. I threw him a quick glance, worried the beast under his skin had forced its way out again, but the demon still wore his human disguise. Only his smoldering eyes seemed otherworldly, the way they seared my flesh as they rested on my chest.

"I wish to see *all* of you, my dove," he purred when my fingers hesitated at my waistline. "Show me what you were willing to sell to save your life."

He didn't have to call me a whore—I still felt the sting of humiliation as I pushed my jeans down my thighs and twisted on the bed to shove them off my legs. I didn't wait for him to request that my panties follow suit.

I curled my legs underneath me and lifted my chin in defiance of the shameful blush spreading all the way from my toes to my hairline when I was finally bared for him. *I* had chosen this. That was something.

Lithely, like a stalking panther, Kurt walked the few steps to the edge of my bed. He reached out to curl his fingers around my chin, and my breath hitched in my throat.

"What a pretty little mortal I've bought," he whispered. There was no softness in his voice, nor in his gaze as he flicked it from my lips to my eyes. "Spread your legs, Emma. Show yourself to me."

I didn't look away from his haunting black eyes as I obeyed his command.

His lip curled as I leaned back on my hands to widen my thighs as far as my tight muscles allowed.

Without a word, he knelt on the floor before me, and my heart thumped uneasily in response. When he reached for my exposed pussy, I had to bite down on my lip to keep my breath from exploding out.

The demon ran his fingers up along my labia, and I clung to the sheets, biting my lip until it bled when he spread me open.

"So, so pretty," he murmured. He flicked his gaze up to mine, letting me see the devilish gleam in those black depths before he leaned in and pressed his mouth to my flesh.

I didn't manage to hold back my breath this time. It came out of my throat in a strangled cry as Kurt kissed me with scalding lips, and zings of pure electricity shot up my spine and into my brain. That was all the warning I had before the demon let out a deep, animalistic groan, wrapped his hands around my thighs to keep me spread open—and devoured me.

I choked out an involuntary moan at the first swipe of his tongue along my inner lips, but it quickly turned to a shriek as he found my clit, closed his lips around it, and *sucked.* Nothing, *nothing* had ever felt like this.

My hands flew to his hair, and I curled up around his head, clinging to him with every ounce of my strength as pleasure so intense it *hurt* tore through my pelvis and lit my entire body on fire.

"Shit, shit, shit!" I fought his grip on my thighs, trying to close them and deny him access even as I ground my hips on his face. "Fuck, oh my God!"

Kurt snarled at my outburst and dug his teeth into my clit. Hard.

I screamed until I thought my vocal cords would break, desperate to break away, but entirely incapable of moving. My pelvis stayed locked in place, and all I could do was throw myself back on the bed and take it. Pain lanced through my entire nervous system, but it came crashing through me on a wave of endorphins laced with ecstasy. Before I even understood what was happening, my muscles locked up and I *came.*

Kurt kept my clit clamped between his teeth, gently working them back and forth over my throbbing nub while I thrashed and howled, any and all ability for coherent speech lost entirely.

He released my poor clit when I had no more left and my climax finally began to wane, giving it a couple of soft licks as I sagged into the mattress, boneless and entirely spent. Only a low-pitched ringing in my ears managed to break through the fog of utter euphoria rolling through my body and mind.

Holy. Shit. If this was the sort of punishment one faced in Hell, maybe I'd sell him my soul after all.

I laughed, the bliss swathing my brain making me see how silly I'd been for being afraid. Painful or not, orgasms as a payment a plan were something I could get behind.

It took a while before my brain came back from orbit long enough for me to realize that I hadn't heard or felt anything from Kurt since he'd eased off my clit.

"Are we good, then? See you in a year?" Lazily, I cracked my eyes open, half-expecting the demon to have poofed into thin air.

He hadn't.

At the foot of my bed, between my still-splayed legs, stood the creature of nightmare from before. Black, curled horns crowned his monstrous features, and reddish-black scales ran down his powerful chest, narrowing at his hips until—

"No!" I gasped my denial out on an exhale, my eyes widening as I stared at his now-naked form. His cock—if something so grotesque could even be called a cock—reached up past his navel, hard and menacing as he loomed above me. It was a dark, unnatural red, the same color as the gleam in his scales, and at least as thick as his wrist. And around the rim of his fat mushroom head, a crown of wicked-looking ridges rode the full circumference.

"I could swathe your mind, darling. Make you beg for it," he purred as he knelt on the mattress. When I tried to close my legs, he grabbed my thighs and kept me open. The heat of his hands traveled up into my pelvis, making my pussy weep despite my terrified whimper. "Take you like I do every other human woman: blinded and high on my magic. But I won't; this was the bargain. I get you just like this—entirely conscious. Raw."

He let one hand slip up higher and trailed a fingertip over my labia. "When you lose yourself to me, there is nothing to hide behind. No pretense. Just you and your little cunt surrendering to a monster."

His touch made me tremble, caught between the physical response his fingers provoked and the terror of my dawning realization of what I'd actually sold him. It wasn't just sex he'd wanted; it was the humiliation and torment of willingly submitting myself to the torture of that cruel cudgel between his thighs.

"I can't," I gasped, unable to hold back the tears stinging my eyes as the full weight of what would happen to my body if he forced that inside of me set in. "Y-You'll rip me apart. I'll die!"

Kurt snorted and glanced down at his menacing cock. White precum pearled at the tip and the bulging veins throbbed—as if his body sensed his nearness to my defenseless sex.

"So *dramatic*," he said, that wicked smirk back on his lips when his burning gaze returned to mine. Without breaking eye contact, he rubbed a thumb over the tip of his cock, gathering precum on the pad. "If I wanted to kill you, there are far more entertaining ways to do so."

I didn't have the strength to pull away when he reached out and smeared the white substance on my trembling bottom lip. My tongue flicked out on instinct, and the taste of him filled my senses. Salty, earthy musk—with just a hint of sulfur.

I wasn't prepared for the primal response from deep in my core. My abdomen cramped, and my pussy fluttered as if grasping for him as liquid gushed out of me and trickled down my ass to soak the mattress.

"Oh!" I croaked, too stunned by my body's response to attempt to close my thighs again when he bent over me.

"No, darling," Kurt rumbled into my ear, his breath raising goosebumps along my neck. "I won't kill you. But I *am* going to open you so, *so* wide—gape that pretty little cunt and make you ride my ridges until you howl for mercy. And then, once I've taken everything, once I've spilled my seed in your womb... one year from now, I'll return. And I will do it all over again."

I stared up at his demonic features, wide-eyed as the added threat sunk in. He would *spill his seed* in me? Was this his true purpose? To make me carry his spawn?

I didn't get to voice the terrifying question. Before I had even fully processed my horror, Kurt reached down between us, and all my thoughts snapped back to the present as the hard, hot head of his cock pressed firmly against my swollen pussy lips.

"Oh!" My hands flew to his shoulders, but even as my mind resisted, my sex softened at the contact, *welcoming* him. Every nerve in my body was tight with anticipation, and where I'd expected nothing but revulsion, there was excitement. He might have been a monster, his very existence might have scared me mindless, but my body...

My body *ached* for him.

Shit, I was so fucked up. I clenched my eyes shut and braced against his shoulders, willing my brain to conjure up an image of what he looked like in his human disguise. Even as I waited for the agony of taking his wicked cock, it helped my mind surrender to my body's demented desires.

Slowly, ever so slowly, Kurt pushed forward. I gasped softly as the pressure of his scalding flesh deepened, splitting my labia apart and threatening entry.

I dug my fingers into his shoulders and tried to submit to his demand. More and more pressure built against my entrance, but he was so *wide,* and my pussy struggled to take even his tip. When the stretching tipped past pleasure, I whimpered and slid my hands down to his stomach to stop his advances.

"I can't. It hurts." Despite my pain, there was no disguising the breathy note to my voice, nor the slick sounds from my eager pussy as Kurt pulled back a few inches, sliding his cock up through my splayed labia.

He dug his sharp teeth into the tender flesh below my ear, gently enough that they didn't pierce the skin, but firmly enough that my nipples pebbled in response.

"Relax," he breathed against my ear, his devious lips brushing over my skin. "Open yourself to me, Emma. It will only hurt for a moment, and then... Then I will make you forget all your fears."

The demon shifted above me, sliding his warm hand down my stomach to my pussy. I gasped when he brushed his fingers over my tight clit, then grunted as he trapped it between two knuckles and squeezed in rapid pulses.

"Oh—*fuck!*" I arched against him without thought, the unrelenting pleasure of his stimulation drowning out my fear of his size. I clawed at his hard abs, any will or ability to stop his penetration lost to the unrelenting desire for another orgasm.

Kurt took advantage of my distraction. Without ever pausing his ministrations on my delicate nub, he pressed his cock to my weeping opening once more—and pushed through.

Sharp pain seared through my taut sheath as he forced my pussy horrifically wide, and I screamed and tried to push him off—but it was too late. His fingers on my clit had me on a knife's edge, and when that thick, brutal head wrenched me open and seated itself inside of me, my entire body seized, and I came so hard black dots danced behind my clenched eyelids.

It hurt—he was too thick, and my spasming muscles clamped vise-like on the wicked ridges along the rim of his cockhead, forcing them deeper into my trembling flesh.

At least they weren't sharp. Some faraway part of my mind capable of more than just screaming was grateful for that. I'd been terrified he'd tear me bloody on those brutal-looking barbs, but where I'd expected bone, they were made from firm cartilage covered in that same silky-soft skin as the rest of his cock.

It took me several long moments to come down from my climax, and then several more to sense anything but white static and that unrelenting fullness just inside my opening. Slowly, so slowly, I became aware of the pressure of the male above me. The warmth of his skin. His bulky muscles wrapped around me. The rasp of his breath in my ear as he panted against me. Fighting to stay in control, I dimly realized.

The realization that he was holding back struck me like a kick in the gut. This monster—this demon—was reining in his own desires in order to let my body adapt to his presence inside of me. He could have shoved in to the hilt as soon as my opening yielded to his mass, and I would have had no choice but to take it. But he hadn't.

Without meaning to, I opened my eyes to look at him.

Black horns glinted in the dim light as he rested his forehead on the mattress next to me. His face, though hardly human, displayed with all possible clarity how much it cost him to hold back. It was twisted in a pained grimace, as if every cell in his preternatural body screamed for him to ravage and *take.* His wide, scaled body trembled, every muscle bulging with strain.

Perhaps it was the haze of orgasm still clouding my mind, but only gratitude filled my chest as I reached out a shaky hand to brush it against his cheek.

The demon's eyes flicked up to mine, and that look stole my breath. I'd known lust before, but *nothing* I'd experienced in my human existence could compare to what I saw in his gaze.

Agony and shock danced in those dark depths, but overriding both was a need so primal it shook me to my core. There was nothing human about this male's desire—yet it made me want to drown in it.

"What are you doing to me, witch?" he snarled, anger in his gravelly voice.

My only response was to twist my neck and place a kiss on his soft lips.

Kurt startled at the brush of my mouth, as if the sensation was entirely alien to him. It only lasted a second. Then he parted his lips and deepened our kiss, making me moan as his taste and ferocity overwhelmed my senses.

Before I could regain my bearings, and without breaking away, Kurt grabbed me by the shoulders, held me in place, and forced his cock all the way in.

"Mmmhhph!" I bit his lips as I tried to scream against the brutal stretch and clawed at his chest in a frantic, instinctive attempt to escape. The demon didn't let me.

He held me steady, growling deep in his throat as his blood dripped into my mouth, and the metallic taste of it rushed my tastebuds as my pussy convulsed around the ruthless cock filling me past full. But despite the expected agony of being opened so roughly, the rush of endorphins was stronger. Underneath this monster, with his gruesome cock pressed firmly against my trembling cervix, I gave in to the madness of pleasure.

"Please, take me. Please! I need you."

Kurt pulled his head back to stare down at me,

raking his burning eyes over my face. Blood dripped from his lips, completing the horror of his monstrous features. But before my hazy gaze, his horns flickered and vanished, dark scales giving way to smooth, pale skin until the only thing inhuman about the creature above me was his jaw-dropping beauty.

I was too far gone to interpret anything in his dark eyes except that same burning desire flaming through my own veins. Groaning out another half-intelligent plea, I tossed my head back into the mattress and braced for what I so desperately needed.

He didn't let me wait long.

Kurt let out a groan, the sound almost pained—and then he pulled his hips back, and my world exploded in a flash of ecstasy.

His cock's ridges dragged against my inner walls, and I *keened* when they dug deep into my G-spot, forcing my entire pelvis to clench on his hard girth.

"F-Fuck!" There was definitely pain this time, but I barely had a chance to register it before Kurt forced his cock deep once more, and my mind blanked.

There was only sensation—only the painfully tight fit of the inhuman cock in my gagging pussy still struggling to take it; only the demon's scalding skin and strong muscles as he grabbed me by the waist and rose over me.

If I'd thought accepting him inside me was

rough, it was nothing compared to taking the fury that was his fucking. He pounded into me with demonic strength, forcing obscene, wet noises from my clinging sheath. His ridges ground on my G-spot with every ruthless thrust, and soon I was struggling not to escape, but to chase yet another climax. I'd never been able to orgasm without having my clit stimulated, but those hellish ridges rode my pussy too hard, Kurt's unrelenting pace giving me no quarter.

Every muscle in my core locked down hard, and I *came.* Howling his name, I ripped bloody streaks down my inhuman lover's broad back, clawing him in mindless fervor as my pussy milked him in fluttering spasms, driving those brutal ridges deeper with every contraction. It *hurt*—it hurt, and it felt *so good,* and there was nothing I could do but cling to him as my body rode an unending torrent of orgasms.

I don't know how long it took before the tether keeping me tied to consciousness frayed down to a single thread, but as red dots danced before my eyes and my vision tunneled, sanity returned long enough for me to realize that if he continued much longer, I would pass out or die from sheer exhaustion.

"Stop... Stop," I managed to gasp, my hoarse voice breaking with the effort. I couldn't even lift my hands to push at his stomach, I was that far gone.

Thankfully, Kurt did stop. With a groan, as if

doing so was physically painful, he paused his merciless pounding, buried all the way inside of me.

I cracked my eyes open, a faint smile of gratitude touching my lips. I was *grateful* he hadn't killed me with too much sex. Some faraway part of my foggy mind did realize how fucked up that was, but I was too high on the pleasure he'd drowned me in to care.

He was staring down at me, his wide chest expanding with every harsh breath, and those deep, dark eyes… they were so full of still-flaming *need,* and my poor pussy contracted weakly on his girth. But there was something else in them too. Horror, or… *awe?*

Before I could even begin to comprehend the motivation behind such emotion, Kurt fell down on top of me and buried his face in the crook of my neck.

"What are you doing to me, woman?" he rasped against my skin, the heat of his breath raising the small hairs there. But he didn't sound angry this time —only bewildered.

"What am *I* doing to *you?*" I said. "I thought you were going to kill me. With your dick!"

His only response was a deep rumble against my ear that made my toes curl, and I wrapped my arms around his wide torso without thinking.

Kurt nuzzled my neck, brushing kisses over the tendon there before he lifted his head and pressed his warm lips to mine.

I hummed mindlessly and opened my mouth for him, my mind fogging over again as I relaxed underneath the demon. I felt so safe—so *protected* in his arms. It was completely illogical, of course; as beautiful as he was in his human form, I hadn't forgotten the horrors of his true nature. But right then, it didn't matter. Nothing but his tongue lazily flicking against mine mattered as my body slowly came down from my orgasm.

Only when he slowly began to rock against me again did my mind snap back from the pleasurable fog.

"No—no more," I pleaded, grimacing as he slowly dragged his ridges over my depleted G-spot. Sensation zinged through my pelvis, but my nerves were too raw for it to be enjoyable this time. "I can't—"

Kurt's only response was to reach a hand between us and rub his index finger over my still-swollen clit.

I mewled in protest and reached down to push him away, but I might as well have tried to shove a mountain. He was so strong, and there was nothing I could do to deter him. He kept stimulating my too-sensitive nub as I clung to his wrist, babbling pleas for him to stop. He only swallowed them with heated kisses until my reluctant body started climbing once more, and my objections slowly turned to hesitant moans.

"There we go, darling," he breathed against me. "One more. I want to feel you come on me as I spill my seed in that pretty little pussy of yours. Give me just one more."

"One more... and you'll stop?" It was meant as a plea, but my voice was husky from mounting pleasure, and when he pressed his thumb firmer on my clit, I dug my nails into his skin with a needy groan.

Instead of answering, Kurt gave me a hard thrust, forcing his cock all the way to my cervix, and I promptly lost any and all ability to negotiate.

Where moments ago his pace had been gentle, he was now anything but. Growling like a beast, he lifted himself over me again, slung my right leg over his shoulder, and fucked me with every ounce of strength in his preternatural body.

I think it hurt, but I wasn't conscious enough to feel it. Throughout the brutal ravaging, Kurt kcpt rubbing my clit, and I came before I could do anything but gasp his name.

And again.

And again.

My pussy fluttered on his pounding cock, and I lost myself until I was nothing but raw flesh and firing nerves. My world was darkness and ecstasy, and I surrendered to it wholly.

Only then—as if he had been waiting for my final submission—did the demon take his climax.

His hands slipped from my pussy and thigh to

my hips, his pace stuttering as he dragged me onto his cock hard and rough once, twice, three times—and then, finally, stilled.

I had expected a roar, or a snarl, but when he released his essence into me, it was with a moan so soft it almost sounded human.

I looked up at him through the blurry haze clouding my vision, shivering at the look of complete reverence on his beautiful face. His eyes were clenched shut, his lips parted around his moans and his head tossed back as his cock pulsed inside of me, his semen coaxed deep by my pussy's rhythmic contractions. It flooded me with warmth, like a soothing balm easing my raw nerves down from the edge of madness until my muscles relaxed and numbness filled my body and mind.

Kurt collapsed on top of me with a groan, pressing his face into the curve of my neck again. But where his skilled lips had tempted and teased before, now he simply breathed with me.

We lay in silence while my brain slowly came back from orbit. Slowly, so slowly, I became aware of the hot weight pressing me into the mattress. His softening presence inside of me faded to a sore throbbing, and the note of sulfur in his musk filled my nostrils as I once again recalled his true features behind that smooth, pale skin.

I had lost myself to a demon.

My breath hitched in my throat, but even

through my mounting discomfort the haze of pleasure softened my rising panic.

Kurt grunted softly against my ear and pulled himself up high enough to lock his gaze on mine. But where I'd expected lecherous triumph, only curiosity shone from his obsidian eyes.

He stared at me in silence for a long moment. Then, without a word, he pushed himself up and off me.

I winced as his still too-thick cock slid from my swollen core, leaving a white trail of semen behind, and fought to push myself up on my elbows so I could watch him.

He moved around my room, pulling on his clothes and shrugging into his black leather jacket last.

He was... leaving? I blinked as he walked to the door, equally relieved and weirdly deflated that this was the end to the most intense night of my life. But this had been our bargain. One night, nothing more.

Hand on the doorknob, Kurt turned to look at me over his shoulder, interrupting my dazed thoughts.

"One year, Emma," he said, and the darkness in his eyes bored into mine, making something in my chest clench as I finally saw the possessiveness flaming there. "I will return for you in one year. And then I will make you my bride."

MORE FROM NORA

We hope you enjoyed ***The Demon's Bargain*** by Nora Ash!

Delve deeper into Nora's dark and sexy demon world in *Demon's Mark.*

Selma Lehmann sees demons. They see her, too.

No one believes that there are monsters walking among us. No one wants to believe.

But they're real, and when Selma falls into Demon Lord Kain's hands, the truth about her curse proves far worse than she could have ever known.

He is ruthlessly handsome, brutally savage—and exactly the fate she's feared since the day she learned what kind of creatures hunt her from the shadows.

He calls her a *Breeder,* and there's only one thing he could want from her...

Nora Ash writes darkly delicious romance with rough and ruthless heroes who just need the right woman to find the man behind the monster.

WWW.NORA-ASH.COM

AN ALPHA FOR THE PACK

BY MEREL PIERCE

AN ALPHA FOR THE PACK

MEREL PIERCE

The communication device on Moira's wrist blared an alert, and the ears of every werewolf in sight flattened with displeasure. She made an apologetic face before hitting the button to accept the page.

"Dawkins, report to briefing room two forthwith."

"Yes, sir."

Moira frowned. The pack of werewolves she'd tended for the past few years had just come back from a mission—a mission where they'd lost their Alpha and team leader, Finn, in an explosion.

Losing Finn wasn't catastrophic, at least not in the way most people would think. The pack would still function as a cohesive, efficient group. But a somber air hung over the werewolves' containment cell. They'd grown to like one another for the most part, Moira thought. She knew they must be sad, even if the only outward signs were drooping ears and sedated demeanors. Comradery seemed to be as strong between the weres as it was between soldiers.

The loss had been hardest on the newest pack member, a young wolf named William, or 28-DPACK, as the ID scrawled on his control collar read. William had only been a were for two cycles, and they had caught him only a few weeks after he'd turned. This had been his first actual mission, and Finn's death weighed heavily on him. He'd been hiding in the den since they'd returned and had grumbled at Moira when she'd tried to talk to him.

Tanner, or 23-DPACK, the tawny second-in-command who was lying on his back with his head in her lap, sighed. Moira tugged the plush fur of his chest between her fingers and looked down into his sea glass-colored eyes. "You'd think they'd have enough decency to let us mourn."

He narrowed his eyes, then sneezed, a sure sign he thought she was being silly.

"Yeah, you're right. Why would they care about that?"

Brande Defenses had forcibly recruited Moira a little over two years ago when she'd peacefully defused a chance encounter with an escaped were. They'd offered her a job, then an ultimatum, then systematically destroyed her life until she had no choice but to agree.

Compared to the weres, she had it easy. As if the curse itself wasn't traumatic enough, Brande Defenses hunted them down and enslaved them with technology so advanced Moira had never seen anything like it. The weres spent ninety-five percent of their lives in a dismal underground facility, only let out for drills or missions. At least Moira had a warm bed and a television to go home to, even if Brande constantly monitored her apartment.

But the ugly truth remained: They were all slaves.

"I guess I'd better go before they send someone down," she murmured. They *would* send someone if she wasn't upstairs in the next ten minutes, and given the agitated state the boys were in, it would only end in pain for the pack. She pushed at Tanner's chest. "If you don't mind?"

The pinched, not quite a snarl wrinkling of his muzzle told her he minded, but Tanner was one of the most levelheaded weres in the group. They both knew what would happen if she took too long. With a grunt, he sat up and leaned against the wall.

Moira stood and squeezed his shoulder as she looked around the enclosure. The three other wolves in sight—Jackson, Danny, and Micha—were trying to rest. A few ears swiveled, and an eye or two slid her way, but no one got up or acknowledged her movements otherwise. It was unlike them.

They were definitely grieving.

She picked her way around the broken-down machinery that served as landscaping and walked to the den at the back. She knew William would have heard the com conversation, but wanted to tell him goodbye anyway. Moira stepped into the dark den, using the wall as guidance, and stopped a few feet away from his outline curled up against the wall.

He was so young, only nineteen when he'd turned. Contrary to what pop culture presented, the curse of a werewolf forced the affected individual to live in their were form twenty-four-seven, only reverting to their human form for brief periods during the full moon. It was a lot for a young man to deal with, and being captured and forced into areas full of gunfire, explosions, and danger—especially when his entire life had already been irrevocably altered by the curse—was a tragedy.

"I've got to go, William," she said. "I just... I just wanted you to know I'll be thinking about you, bud."

She waited for a few seconds, but he didn't respond. She knew he'd heard her, though, and that would have to do.

Moira sped through the enclosure, slowing as she passed the others. She wanted to say something about Finn, but condolences seemed so shallow. Her throat tightened as she looked her boys over, her eyes prickling with heat. She'd put so much blood, sweat, and tears into bonding with them. They were *hers*, yet Brande could separate them on a whim. The thought made her sick to her stomach.

"I'll try to come back as soon as I can, guys."

Tanner chuffed and jerked his chin in acknowledgement, the corner of his lip lifting in a faint smile, albeit a sad one. Moira cleared her throat and waved as she resumed her walking. She didn't bother to check whether anyone was watching as she punched in her code; they all knew there was no escaping this facility, and they wouldn't risk putting her in harm's way to try.

The first set of secure doors opened, and she passed through into the waiting dock. The doors closed behind her before the light flashed green above her head. She removed the collar controller from her wrist and hung it up, then picked up her badge and slipped it around her neck. After she flashed it in front of the reader at the opposite end of the room, the reinforced doors slid back, revealing the stairs that would take her to the observation deck above the enclosure.

The trip through the dismal lower levels to the whitewashed upper floors took only a few minutes, but it was long enough for her to start worrying about what her boss wanted. They rarely ever called her in outside of their weekly briefings. It might be about Finn, but she doubted it. She'd never lost one of her own pack before, but other people had, and her general impression was that management just went on like said man/were had never existed.

She paused outside the briefing room, taking a deep breath and squaring her shoulders before stepping through the door. The men in this facility were impossibly chauvinistic and elitist, but appearing demure or agreeable didn't win a woman any points with them. She always tried to hold her own and not let them affect her, even if she didn't have the same training or experience they did. After all, they wanted her enough to threaten her livelihood if she didn't work for them, so she was obviously an asset, despite how they treated her.

Two men sat at the long rectangular table: her supervisor, Richard Mooreland, and the manager of the facility, Patrick North. Moira swallowed hard. Goosebumps prickled her skin as unease settled in her stomach. She rarely saw the facility manager. He only came down from his office when serious shit went wrong. This couldn't be good.

Her supervisor motioned at the seat across from him. "Have a seat, Dawkins."

"Thank you, sir."

She sat, glancing back and forth between the two men cautiously. Try as she might, Moira couldn't think of a single reason for them to call her that required North's attention. She had no clue what was going on.

Thankfully, they didn't make her wait long.

"I'm sure you're wondering why we called you in," North began, scrutinizing her as he lifted a remote and pointed it over his shoulder. With the press of a button, the screen behind him lit with the image of a large silver were in harsh restraints, his body stretched out next to several pairs of boots. He looked dead, or sedated. "He is why."

Moira frowned as she studied the image. It was difficult to say for sure since he was on the ground, but she'd swear this werewolf was bigger than any of her boys. He had stockier muscles and a blockier head, making him more tank-like than "lean and mean." He also had a thick ruff of fur around his neck and shoulders that reminded her of a lion. She hadn't seen such features before, which made her wonder why he was so different.

"He's a recent acquisition," North finally continued. "He has a lot of potential, but his acclimation to the program has been less than stellar."

"He's a pain in the ass," her boss interjected. "We've already had some serious injuries and one fatality."

"The normal methods of subduing new inductees haven't been as effective on him as they have on prior subjects." North rubbed his balding head and pushed his glasses up on his nose. "I want him in the program, but if we can't get him under control, he isn't worth shit to us. That's where you come in."

"Me?" Moira played dumb, but she suspected what they wanted, and she didn't feel good about it. They'd brought in a were they couldn't control, one who already had at least one fatality under his belt, and they wanted her to... what? Make friends?

"You're the only handler in the facility who hasn't suffered anything more serious than some bruises and scrapes," Mooreland scoffed. "You make it look easy, considering you don't have any sort of military or leadership background."

"Yes," North agreed, nodding as he glanced in Mooreland's direction. "There's something about your way of handling them that even the other female caretakers can't replicate. It may not make sense to me, but there's no arguing with results. When it comes to behavior modification, you have the highest success rate of all time."

Moira knew saying no wasn't an option. As much as she'd have liked to avoid the situation altogether, she couldn't bear to think about what they would do to him if he didn't assimilate. The facility only viewed them as animals, but Moira knew better. The man was still there, lurking beneath the surface.

She sucked in a fortifying breath and glanced at the picture again. "What do we know about him?"

"Nothing," North snapped.

"Nothing?" Moira glanced between the two men. They never knew *nothing* about the weres—they tracked potential targets for weeks before taking them. There was always something—a missing persons report coinciding with the were's appearance in the area; a new were returning home and leading them to his identity—never *nothing*. "Where did he come from?"

"Appalachia," Mooreland answered. "Took us three months to catch the bastard. He was hard to find."

"How long have they been reporting sightings?" Moira queried as her gaze drifted back to the screen. He looked rough. Whether it was from the facility's handling or his way of life, she didn't know, but his coat was tousled and missing in places, rust-colored stains clinging to his fur in others.

"Sporadic, but at least fifteen years, according to locals."

"Fifteen ye—" The words died in her throat. Moira knew the scope of the Brande project was small, considering how large the country was, but she'd never heard of a were surviving so long. Normally they caused enough destruction to get themselves eliminated long before the decade mark. Even the oldest subjects in the facility hadn't been were longer than a few years before they were captured.

"What about missing persons reports in the area?"

"There are fifteen adult males that have gone missing in a fifty-mile radius since the first reported sighting." North pushed a piece of paper across the table to her. "I think you understand the real scope of the problem now. He's rather feral, and determining his identity has been more difficult than usual."

"But he's restrained," Mooreland added. "You won't be in any danger. More than anything, we're just curious how he'll respond to you. If his reaction is favorable, we'll move forward. If not, we'll dispose of him."

"I see." She hated how callously they spoke about the weres, but tried to mask her disapproval. "When did you want me to see him?"

"Now," the two men answered in unison.

"I'm tired of his bullshit," North continued. "If he won't show progress, we need to make space for another candidate." He folded his hands on the table and waited for her response.

Moira tried to swallow her concerns and find the courage to agree as she looked over the missing persons list and the tiny pictures next to the names. Knowing he'd killed someone and might be feral was terrifying. The weres were unpredictable enough as it was. She'd been terrified of being gutted or raped the first few months she'd worked with the pack, since they'd often fought over her. But they seemed like puppies compared to this wolf.

"Okay. I should probably shower and change, though, since I've been with the pack. It might agitate him."

"We don't have time for that nonsense, Dawkins," Mooreland interjected, a frown etched across the hard lines of his face. "Like I said, he's bound. You'll be fine. It's now or never."

The push made her feel even more uncomfortable about the situation, but there was nothing to be done. Moira folded the piece of paper and stuck it in her pocket. "All right. I'd like to take something high-value down with me. Some organ meat, maybe? Just in case he responds favorably."

"He's muzzled," North informed her. "Won't do you much good."

"I'd like permission to remove the muzzle, then, if I feel comfortable with it. If he's bound, it should be fine. I won't if I don't like his body language."

"You want to take that risk, that's your choice. We'll be down with a few men shortly. We'll monitor from the observation deck. If things go south, we'll intervene. He's on B Level in containment cell four."

The men both stood, and Moira took it as her cue to leave.

The walk to the freezer and then to his cell was fraught with worries and failed attempts to develop a plan of action. It was going to be harder to read his body language with him bound, but she hoped she could make enough progress with him to save his life.

Her keycard granted her access to the observation deck above his cell, and Moira stopped to assess the situation before she went down. Just like they'd said, he was stretched out and bound by metal containment bands that could only be released remotely via a coded entry.

They'd laid him on his belly with his steel-cage muzzle plastered to the floor, his arms bound to his torso at his shoulders, chest, and waist, and his legs banded at his thighs, knees, and ankles. He was huge, easily double the size of her boys.

It was a miserable-looking position, and Moira had no trouble envisioning them dumping him on the floor and leaving him how he lay with no concern for his comfort.

Sighing, she turned away from the window and made her way through the next door and down the stairs to the entrance of his pen. Moira left her badge and picked up the remote for his correction collar, then coded the door that would release her into the enclosure.

As the door rolled back, he erupted in a vicious, bone-jarring growl. His ears pressed flat against his skull as the eye facing her rolled in her direction. Through the steel basket of his muzzle, she saw the wicked white of his teeth as he snarled. It was a convincing threat, even with him bound. Moira hesitated a second before she forced herself to step over the threshold.

His noise was deafening, rattling through the space and echoing off the walls above. Knowing it would be impossible for him to hear her until he stopped, she lifted her hands, made eye contact briefly, and then averted her gaze again. She showed him her palms as she edged closer, a bucket of meat dangling from the crook of her elbow.

She stayed in the center of his left eye's field of vision so he didn't think she was trying to sneak around him. Seven feet away, she stopped, unable to make herself get closer. She knelt and sat back on her heels, slowly relaxing her arms and setting the bucket down beside her. Then she folded her hands in her lap and waited.

Moira glanced up periodically, but never held his gaze. She didn't want to challenge him when he already felt threatened.

She wasn't sure how long it took for the growling and snarling to wane. Ten minutes? Fifteen? She waited until the noise died down to wary bursts before she tried to engage.

Moira finally allowed herself to meet his gaze, though she kept her head angled down and her posture neutral.

"I know what you're thinking," she murmured, "but I will not hurt you. I have the controller for your collar, but I *don't* want to use it, and I don't have any other weapons. I just want to talk to you."

He huffed at her, but his growling stuttered to a stop.

Moira sighed in relief and nodded. "Good. That's good. I brought you something to eat, but I can't take off your muzzle until I know you a little better, so I'd like us to talk awhile first."

He narrowed his eye and sneezed, which Moira recognized from her time with the other wolves as an expression of skepticism.

"Oh, I know you can't talk, but we can still communicate. I'll ask you yes or no questions, and to answer, you can put your ears forward for yes or grunt for no. Does that work?"

He angled his head in her direction, far enough she could see both icy-blue irises scrutinizing her instead of just one. A few seconds passed in silence, and Moira wondered if he even understood her, until the triangular ears released from their pinned position and pivoted to face her. Just as quickly, they snapped back against his skull.

Moira smiled again.

"Good. I'm glad." She relaxed a little, settling into her position. "Has anyone explained why you're here?"

He grunted, shifting uncomfortably as he focused on her.

Moira bit back another smile, glad he was cooperating, but not wanting him to think she enjoyed what she had to say.

"I'm sorry. They seem to forget there's still a man in there under all that fur." She took a deep breath, readying herself for the explanation. "This facility is... Well, I guess it's a weapons technology company. For the past eight years, they've captured and trained werewolves for specific operations. There are three teams right now; each one is hired out for missions. Sometimes it's government, sometimes its private sector, but basically, you guys are like... attack dogs on steroids. Besides missions and training, the weres live here in the facility. Understand?"

He wrinkled his muzzle, flicked his ears forward, then pressed them back.

"I won't lie to you—werewolves who don't assimilate into the program are disposed of. They don't want assets they can't control. Right now, that's what you are: an asset they can't control. They want you in the program, but not if you're killing employees and being combative."

He interrupted her with a guttural growl. Moira swallowed hard and nodded, trying not to let the vicious noise affect her. "No, I understand. It's a screwed-up situation. No one deserves to have their freedom taken away. It's not ideal by any means, but some of the boys... some weres, I mean... they enjoy the work. It's better than being dead, right?"

Other than continuing to rumble at her, he didn't respond.

Moira gave him a few minutes to come to terms

with the news before she spoke again. When he heaved a sigh, Moira glanced up.

"I wasn't trying to upset you. I just wanted to be honest. But why don't we talk about something else for a while?"

He snarled and turned his head, looking straight ahead instead of toward her. It was discouraging, but Moira wasn't ready to give up yet.

She grabbed the bucket and scooted closer on her knees, inching forward until only five feet separated them instead of seven. He shot her a look once or twice, but didn't respond otherwise. Obviously, he didn't see Moira as a threat.

"They said they found you in Appalachia. Is that where you're from?" She scooted a little closer, leaning to catch his eye. "I know you're upset, but please... talk to me. I've already lost someone today. I don't want to lose anyone else."

She hadn't expected her voice to hitch when she mentioned losing Finn, but her throat tightened and her eyes burned, making her wish she'd had time to grieve before meeting this new were. She hadn't cried around the boys because she'd wanted to be strong for them, so sadness sat heavy in her chest. Moira cleared her throat and blinked away her pending tears.

He was staring again, his expression hovering between suspicion and guarded curiosity.

"Finn, the Alpha of the pack I take care of...

died," she explained. "Sorry. It just happened. I guess I haven't had time to cope with it yet. He was a good man. The pack and I are going to miss him."

The massive were let out a weary sigh, metal grating on the concrete floor as he shifted again, the tension leaving his form as he watched her. Recognizing he'd softened at her confession, Moira tried again.

"I know you don't know me from Adam, but the weres aren't the only ones trapped. I am too. The situation sucks for all of us. But I've tried to make a difference, make things better for them. I'd like to make things better for you too, if you'll let me."

He didn't signal yes, but he didn't grunt either. Moira decided it was good enough. Slowly she pulled the list of names from her back pocket, holding it out so he could see it was only paper. "I asked if you were from Appalachia because I'd like to call you by your name, but I have to figure out who you are to do that. This is a list of missing persons reports over the last fifteen years, all within a fifty-mile radius of where they found you. Most weres stay close to home after they change."

Moira unfolded the paper, clasping it between her hands as she split her attention between the marked names on the paper and him. "I just want to know your name so I can address you properly. It's safe to tell me. The only reason they care about who you were is so they can check your background for military training or other experience they think could be useful to them. They won't contact anyone from your life before you were a werewolf."

She knew explaining things could seem just as suspicious as silence, but she hoped transparency would make the difference. It was a risk, but she had little to lose.

"I'm going to read off the names. If you hear yours, signal yes for me?"

The were heaved another agitated sigh, but his ears flickered forward. Moira smiled.

"William Michaelson." She paused and glanced up to check for a response, but he gave none. "David Townlin."

Moira repeated the process eight more times with no reaction from him, but the ninth name, Joseph Hunt, caught his attention. His eyes widened and his ears came up sharply, though she suspected it hadn't been intentional. She glanced back down at the paper. Joseph Hunt had been thirty-seven years old when he'd vanished from his cabin in Virginia, where he lived alone. An older sister had reported him missing.

"Is that you? Joseph Hunt?"

His ears stayed pricked, but his expression was hard to read. Moira continued. "That was fifteen years ago... You've been out there alone all this time?"

He was still staring, his ears still pointed in her direction.

"I'm going to assume that means yes."

She shuffled forward, tugging her bucket along with her. Three feet away, she paused again. "That's a really long time to be alone," she said, schooling her tone to sound sympathetic. "You can obviously take care of yourself, but that still must have been hard."

Slowly he folded his ears back, but didn't grunt. Given how he was studying her, Moira knew something was bothering him, so she tried to guess at what.

"I can try to find out about your sister," she volunteered cautiously, not wanting to upset him. "You know, see if she's still living, see what kind of life she led—if she was happy. I'm sure she's missed you... But it would be nice to know if things turned out okay for her, right?"

He grunted, his expression darkening.

"No? Okay." Moira edged closer, mindful of how intensely he watched her movements. Despite his displeasure, the hostility they'd started with was no longer rolling off him, which made her tentatively optimistic. "If you ever change your mind though, just let me know."

Now only a foot away, Moira stopped again, but this time, she didn't sit back. She glanced at the observation deck, relieved to see the green light above the two-way glass. The light wouldn't be lit if the room beyond was empty, even if she couldn't see through it. It gave her the confidence to continue.

"I'd really like to take the muzzle off and give you something to eat. Can I trust you? I know you must be hungry."

His ears flicked forward again. Admittedly, Moira had reservations about trusting him. He'd been more cooperative than she'd expected, almost too much, but she wanted a positive rapport with him. The food would help, especially since she'd have to handfeed him because of his positioning.

"Okay, let's give this a try, then." She leaned forward, keeping her arms raised in case she needed to escape his gnashing teeth. The metal bands were so tight she had to dig her fingers into his fur to get a good hold on the clasps, and she winced as she tugged at the pieces, trying to get it loose. "Sorry, it's really tight. Hang on."

She abandoned her plans of keeping distance between them, needing her knees on either side of his nose to get enough leverage to pop the clasp. Joseph didn't move. Moira hooked a finger into the metal basket and shuffled back before pulling it off his face and pushing it away.

The second it came off, he shook his head, snarling and licking his muzzle. It wasn't hard to see why—the short, dense fur along the bridge of his snout was ruffled, and several creases marked where the metal basket had pressed into his skin. Moira wrinkled her nose.

"I guess they didn't expect anyone with a head your size when they designed those. Most of the werewolves here are smaller than you."

Joseph grunted and sneezed, side-eyeing her as she reached for her bucket.

"I'll have to feed you by hand, I guess. They left you in an odd position." She pulled out the largest piece of the cow liver she'd cut, holding it between two fingers. Moira tried to breathe evenly as she lowered it toward his muzzle, but dismay rose in her chest as her hand trembled so hard the meat shook. Thankfully, he either didn't notice or didn't care.

Joseph angled his head and opened his mouth for the liver, which Moira dropped once it was so close he couldn't miss. His jaw snapped shut like a steel trap and she jumped, her cheeks heating with embarrassment.

The meat disappeared in seconds, so Moira reached into the bucket for another, and then another, until he'd eaten fifteen pounds of meat and the bucket was empty. The expectant glance he gave the bucket after she'd fed him the last piece made her feel bad.

"Sorry, Joseph. That's all I have for now."

She lowered her hands to her knees, palms up to prevent the blood on her fingers from getting on her clothes, and smiled at him. Joseph angled his head toward her, and before she could react, his tongue darted out against her fingers. Moira startled at the warm drag against her skin. He paused with his tongue pressed to her palm, his pretty ice-blue eyes focused on her.

Moira's cheeks warmed. "Sorry. Little jumpy today, I guess."

Unbothered, he resumed his licking until her hands were clean. When he stopped, she held them up and inspected them. "Thanks. At least I don't have to worry about getting my pants dirty now."

Moira assessed him more closely now that the threat of violence had waned. His tangled coat was matted with old blood, scabs, and refuse from the forest. Scars dissected his muzzle, ear tips, and scattered over the rest of his body. Whether they were new or old was hard to say, since weres healed so quickly. She hated to see his beautiful fur in such a condition.

She always helped the boys with grooming when they returned from missions; it was part of their routine, how she bonded with them. They'd bathed before she'd met them, but brushing their coats or tails didn't seem to have crossed their minds until she'd suggested it. Being men, she doubted they'd prioritized grooming in their human lives, and it certainly wasn't on their minds as wolves. But they enjoyed it when *she* did it.

"I don't think you're feral," she murmured,

resisting the urge to bury her fingers in his ruff. "I think you just don't tolerate assholes."

He chuffed, a sound weres made to show their amusement, and Moira felt a smile forming without her permission.

Joseph turned his attention to sniffing her knees, which he could barely reach with the tip of his nose, and the hot puffs of air against the fabric made goosebumps rise along her arms. His ears tipped her direction and his pupils dilated as he snuffled at her, and a chill slid up Moira's spine. He was scenting the other weres on her, and she recognized the intensity of his expression.

The twigs trapped in his tail scratched against the concrete as it lashed to life, a quick flick that made the hair on the back of her neck rise in warning. *Overstimulation.* Moira leaned back slowly.

"I think maybe it's time I—"

The intercom crackled to life over the enclosure, stopping her words midstream. Joseph snarled, his head whipping toward the noise.

"Excellent progress, Dawkins. Let's move to the next stage."

Moira's eyes widened in disbelief, panic swelling as she scrambled to her feet. "No, he's not ready yet!"

"We told you, it's now or never. We don't have time to take it slow."

A choir of electronic beeps erupted behind her, and Moira's heart sank. One after the other, the pressurized clasps disengaged, and the riot of clattering metal and flurry of motion that followed cemented what they had done.

They'd released him.

Afraid to move, Moira clenched her hands at her sides and kept still. It was hard to ignore the instinct to run, but she knew better. He'd give chase, and she didn't know him well enough to say how it would end. She felt him step up behind her, the heat of his massive body bleeding through her clothing even though he hadn't touched her.

His head descended over her shoulder, cheek bumping the side of her head as he lowered his muzzle to her throat and inhaled a noisy breath. Moira's heart fluttered with anxiety as he scented her, knowing how badly things could go.

She'd been in this situation before, at the mercy of a were whose animal instincts were more likely to take charge because of overstimulation. Moira thought she might have been able to fully defuse him, had her bosses not chosen that exact moment to speak up and release him. The presence of the men who'd hurt him and were keeping him here had only agitated him, and combined with the scent of the other weres on her, it was proving to be a tough challenge for him to overcome. Weres were territorial by nature, and when confined, they exerted their dominance over whatever they could—other weres, guards, and even handlers like Moira. It was their way of trying to maintain control where they had none.

Joseph rumbled—a low, throaty noise like the purring of a large feline—and stepped in front of her. He was so tall Moira was only eyelevel with his sternum now that he was free of his bonds, bipedal and moving upright like a man. He blocked out everything behind him, including her view of the observation deck.

"Joseph..." Moira lifted her eyes to meet his gaze and kept her posture neutral. Purring was something weres did when they were aroused or feeling affectionate. Considering the situation, Moira was betting it was the former. "Please... try to calm down."

He stepped forward, forcing her to shuffle back. He sucked in another lungful of her scent and resumed rumbling as he took another step toward her, and then another, herding Moira away from the center of the room toward the back of the enclosure.

Where the den was.

Moira knew where this was heading. Sensibly, she knew she still had the control to his collar around her wrist, but they'd said the normal methods of behavior modification hadn't worked with him, and if she corrected him and it didn't work, he'd only be angry.

Moira didn't want to call out for help, either. She knew what they'd do to him, and she couldn't bear the idea of witnessing it, let alone being responsible for it.

"I can guess what you're thinking, but they don't care if you do that to me. It won't matter to them. Can we please just keep talking? We were doing well before they showed up, weren't we?"

He chuffed and dipped his head, his eyes never leaving hers. She knew he understood, but it didn't seem to matter. He'd tolerated enough—enough pain, enough misery, enough not being in control.

Joseph continued to force her backward, angling this way or that to move her beyond whatever obstacles blocked their path. Too soon, her back bumped against the faux rock wall outside the den. He grabbed her upper arm with clawed, rough-padded fingers and pushed her toward the entrance. He wasn't delicate about it, but he wasn't cruel either. Once they were inside the relative darkness of the den, he crowded her against the wall and got down on his knees in front of her. Even then, he was still almost as tall as Moira.

It happened in such a hurry Moira had no time to react. The button from her pants pinged off a nearby wall as he yanked her jeans and panties down over her hips, jerking her forward and forcing her to put her hands on his shoulders to steady herself. The stinging tracks along her hips and thighs told her his nails had left their marks on her skin, furrows made even more obvious when he stopped to inspect the thin red lines blooming on her flesh.

Moira took a shaky breath as he darted out his tongue and dragged it up the front of her thigh, tracing the trail one of his nails had left. She tried to ignore the way the sensation made her stomach clench. He repeated the action, inching closer to the apex of her thighs with each stroke.

"Joseph, please. Don't do this," Moira whispered urgently. She gripped his shoulders and tried to push him back, but he didn't move. Instead he started purring again as he worked his way to her center with his wide, rough tongue.

She sent an anxious glance toward the den entrance, but there was no one there—and no sign that anyone was coming. They must have known what he intended when he'd dragged her back here, but they appeared to be waiting for her to give the word before they intervened. If they did, Moira thought it likely that Joseph, and maybe some guards, would end up dead. She didn't want that.

Was saving him worth letting him assault her? Moira's heart hurt at the idea of him being murdered over something she knew he couldn't help. Weres were so primal that their animal instincts were often impossible for the man within to override.

But she didn't know what to expect. How seriously could he hurt her? She wasn't sure. The boys in her pack were more well-endowed than most human men, from what she'd seen, but their excitement had often revealed a more concerning quirk of their anatomy: a knot the size of a baseball that swelled at the base of their cocks. And Joseph? Joseph was so much bigger...

His wide, flat tongue pushed between the folds of her sex and rasped up over her clit, derailing her thoughts. Moira shuddered and twitched, going up on her tiptoes to escape the sensation as he repeated the action, forcing her entire body to flush with warmth.

Moira dug her nails into his shoulders and tried to wriggle away, only to have him clamp his hands over her hips and push his tongue so deep he penetrated her tight channel with it. She yelped at the foreign sensation as he dragged it over her sensitive inner tissues, and to her shame, her body responded with a rush of fluid that only seemed to encourage him. Before long she was panting and twitching under the onslaught, biting her tongue against the swell of an orgasm.

She choked on a moan as pleasure broke over her in an unsettling wave, hoping no one beyond the blessedly unmonitored den would hear. The orgasm left her quivering and using his shoulders for support.

Joseph continued his leisurely torture until her hips were jerking with every lap of his tongue, her skin too sensitive to bear it any longer.

"Please, I can't. No more," she panted, shaking her head and staring up at the dark ceiling. Joseph chuffed at her, but his tongue retreated. Moira might have felt relief, if he hadn't shuffled back and pulled her to her knees in front of him before she had the chance to gather her wits.

With one massive hand, he pulled her down by her nape, forcing her to brace her weight on the heels of her hands as he lowered his free hand to his groin. Moira's eyes widened as her gaze followed its path, struck speechless at the sight of what waited there.

With his hips angled, the light from the entrance exposed the deep plum-colored cock erect and proud between his thighs. She'd never seen anything like it. As opposed to the sleek, tapered head she'd seen on other were cocks, his was round and wide like a battering ram, with a slightly flared, ridge-marked edge. A clear fluid was already dripping steadily from its tip, glistening in the dim light. It looked thick and viscous, like honey.

The shaft itself flared just behind the head, widening for several inches in a bulbous shape that progressed to a matching, but slightly larger bulge just below it. It almost looked as if he had two knots in his shaft, which were already expanding. There was no other way to describe it. He closed his fingers around the base, and Moira's mouth ran dry.

He urged her forward by her nape while his hips rolled up, bringing his monstrous cock within inches of her face. He started purring again as he guided her, but Moira whined in protest. Her cheeks burned hot as she glanced up at him, ashamed to admit she *was* curious. Joseph only dipped his chin and continued to rumble encouragement.

She touched him, her fingers fluttering lightly over the head and down his shaft. He was so hot—silky and hot. Moira stroked his shaft a few times, testing the sensations and gauging his responses. A quick glance toward the entrance to the den told her they were still alone, so she grew a little braver. She leaned forward and closed her mouth over his tip, her tongue darting out to test the sticky wetness gathered there.

Her senses buzzed as the flavor washed over her tastebuds, his flavor nothing like she'd expected—musky but clean, with the faintest hint of sweetness. She opened her mouth wider, pressing her tongue flat as she tried to spread her lips around his girth.

His purr took on a darker edge, and he gave a small, brisk thrust, stretching her lips wide over the head of his cock as he held her in place. Moira shuffled closer, leaning forward to secure both hands around his shaft as she lapped and sucked at his tip, working him as best she could.

Above her head, Joseph grunted and huffed, his hips moving with an ever-increasing urgency as she caressed him with hand and mouth alike. Moira's reservations bled away under his noises of praise and encouragement as he stroked her hair with surprising gentleness. It had been so long since she'd been with a man—two years, in fact. Ever since she'd started with the program. She'd forgotten how good it felt to be on her knees, sucking a cock she knew would soon fill her in the way she needed most.

When he pulled her off moments later, she glared at him, confused and annoyed. His eyes glinted and he flashed a toothy grin at her, the sight of his teeth sending a trill of excitement and nervousness straight to her core. His intentions became obvious when he rearranged her, moving her to face the wall and shuffling close behind her, putting himself between her and the entrance to the den.

Moira couldn't move. He'd never removed her pants, only lowered them, trapping her knees and calves with the bunched fabric. So when he slid a hand beneath her belly and pulled her ass up while pushing her head onto the floor with his free hand, Moira was at his mercy.

He pressed his shaft into the crease between her ass cheeks, nestling the heavy, slick weight of it there. Her heart stuttered when he rolled his hips, sliding his cock back and forth.

"I don't think I can, Joseph," she whispered anxiously. "You're so big..."

But he wasn't listening. He rolled his hips back and angled his cock down so his head split the soaked lips of her sex as he kept thrusting. Back and forth he teased her, rubbing his hot flesh over her sensitive skin.

He palmed her ass, covering both globes with his massive hands, and used his thumbs to pull her cheeks apart. Moira hissed when he notched himself at her entrance, panic lancing through her chest as her body tensed for pain.

As he eased his hips forward, the flaring tip of his cock gave way, folding back against his shaft and easing his invasion. Even so, his unnatural heat and massive girth made Moira break out in a cold sweat.

Joseph slowly worked himself into her body with more care than she'd thought possible. She forced herself to breathe through the strain, but she was trembling by the time he was half-seated and down to the second bulge in his shaft.

His body temperature was so high, she could feel every little change inside her body. She could feel his cock kicking and releasing little jets of lubricant. The hot fluid leaked out around his cock, dripping from her sex and trailing down her thighs. Moira should have felt embarrassed and humiliated, but there was something so dirty about the situation that she knew it wasn't only his arousal leaking from her.

Her body rocked forward as he tried to push deeper, but gaining ground was getting harder the deeper he plunged. Joseph grabbed her hips, holding her steady as he surged forward with increasing force.

Moira swallowed a yelp and pinched her eyes closed against the discomfort. Her inner tissues burned as he forced his way deeper, his hips jerking faster and rougher, until she was stretched around the widest part of his shaft. She panted and squirmed, trying to get away from the pressure, but he was unrelenting.

"Please..." she whined, trying to twist so she could see him. "It's too much... I can't."

His purr filled the den, reassurance resonating off the walls as he tightened his grip on her hips. Before she could protest, he gave a brutal thrust, forcing her the rest of the way down his bulging cock.

She clamped her hands over her mouth to smother her pained cry. Stars danced in her vision, and for a moment, she thought she'd faint. The pain was intense—a burning, throbbing invasion she couldn't escape—especially now with the widest part lodged inside her. The thought of pulling herself off the gigantic knot made her stomach roll.

He stilled, leaning over her to nudge her cheek with his nose. Moira nodded to signal she was okay, but didn't dare remove her hands from her mouth. She didn't trust herself to be quiet when he thrust again.

To her surprise, he didn't move for several moments. His tongue darted out against her cheek and throat as he nuzzled her, cooing against her skin.

His distraction worked, easing her pain and loosening the tightness in her lungs. She forced herself to relax, and parted her fingers over her lips to take a deep breath.

Joseph cooed, and with a final approving lick over her throat, he straightened and rolled his hips, the roughened fur of his pelvis grinding against her ass. Moira gasped at the fresh burst of sensation, but the discomfort was easier to bear. Him not drawing back on the bulging shaft was a relief. Instead, he ground himself inside her.

Warmth bloomed in her core, spreading through her body as the pain of his initial invasion morphed into pleasure. His cock pulsed inside her, every tiny ridge along its head rubbing sensitive nerves in her channel, the ever-swelling shaft filling her to overflowing. It was unlike anything Moira had experienced before.

Being filled by him, bred by him, was a primal experience—violating, frightening, and intensely erotic.

Joseph stilled, his cock rippling and twitching inside her. His nails bit into the soft flesh of her hips as his orgasm erupted. Her insides heated and tingled under the sensation of him bathing them with his cum, and the growing pressure in Moira's belly broke as her own pleasure crested.

A whirring noise broke through her reverie, and Moira yelped when Joseph shifted to look behind him at the entrance to the den. The low growl that rumbled up from his chest told her their private moment had been interrupted, and by a drone, from the sound of it. Moira couldn't see it, thankfully; Joseph's body shielded her from that particular humiliation. The knowledge that everyone would now know without question what had happened in the den with the feral were made her cheeks burn hot.

North's voice crackled out of the speaker on the bottom of the drone, cold and smug. "Well, Dawkins, looks like your pack has a new Alpha."

MORE FROM MEREL

We hope you enjoyed ***An Alpha for the Pack*** by Merel Pierce!

Continue the world of Merel Pierce in *Claiming His Myshka.*

Being the Omega of the Asbury syndicate isn't as glamorous as some might think.

Aislin would like nothing more than for someone to rescue her from the cruelty of the Alpha who force bonded her and made her his pet.

When a new Alpha comes to town claiming he wants to do business with the syndicate, Aislin senses danger.

He isn't here just for business. He's here for her.

Merel Pierce writes sexy bad-boys, dangerous mafia men, and all varieties of Omegaverse men.

WWW.RETICENTDESIREPUBLICATION-
S.COM/MEREL-PIERCE

DOMINATING THE DEMIGODDESS

BY OPHELIA BELL

DOMINATING THE DEMIGODDESS

OPHELIA BELL

THE FACT that I woke up this morning with the urge to sing should have been my first warning the day would take an unexpected turn. When you're a demigoddess whose sole purpose in life is to torment her worshippers with cryptic riddles, and who thrives on sodomizing them for the privilege of receiving such riddles, *singing* ruins the effect. I don't want them in thrall to me, after all; I want them to experience every deliciously naughty second of the things I do to them.

But this morning, my gem-encrusted pool sparkles more brightly in the sunbeams streaming down from the grotto's skylight above. The cool water laps at the tips of my many tails where they drape over the edge of the mossy ledge I call a bed. When I slip into the refreshing depths, each tail finds purchase beneath, carrying me into the center, where I await the first soul who might brave the path into my cave. They will strip bare in order to gain an audience with me, because there are no lies within the bounds of my powerful aura.

All who enter must show their true selves, and thus I am never surprised by what I see. And they all submit to me to gain what bits of wisdom I choose to share. They call me an oracle, a legend among the higher races, a being of immense power born of a union between *three* gods: Gaia, the Mother Dragon, and Dionysus, who shared their essences with one another to prove that Fate does not hold all the cards.

I am the product of that divine triad.

I am the Diviner.

But *what* I am is *hungry*, so I wish the first penitent of the day would hurry up and get here so I can have my breakfast. I continue to hum as I bathe. The priestesses visit weekly and leave me sweet soaps and soft cloths, and I take full advantage today, because for some reason, today feels special.

Each tail receives my full attention, and I work my way up from there. I am nothing if not fastidious about my appearance. My scales shine when I'm done, my pale gray-green skin glistens, and the writhing tendrils on my head nip at my fingers with their sharp little teeth when I pour water over them to rinse away the suds.

Next I stretch and flex each tail to warm up. Sometimes the penitents arrive in groups, so I have to be prepared to initiate multiple people at once. If they're nymphs, they have more orifices to invade while I extract my payment from them. For the satyrs, I need my smaller tails to be limber enough to stroke their throbbing cocks while I violate them with the larger ones.

Some resist, but all eventually surrender. I never cause pain unless they ask for it. *Every* visitor leaves my lair satisfied on multiple levels. You would think they'd visit more often.

I'm so lost to my song I almost miss the low rumble of the earth around me, but the vibrations make my hair stand on end, every tendril writhing and snapping at the air. I go still, the cloth poised between my breasts. The surface of the water stills with me.

Then it comes again—a single footstep, but one from a being powerful enough to make the bedrock beneath my cave shake.

My heart skips a beat. Nothing that powerful has *ever* entered my grotto before. Can a creature that potent even fit through the narrow passageway?

In my periphery I catch sight of four Fate hounds, flickering wildly in and out like purple mirages, chasing their own tails or digging in unseen dirt. Their presence sends my pulse skyrocketing. It isn't possible—Fate has no jurisdiction over me.

Except what if it isn't Fate? There is another who commands the hounds, and I know her story.

She has become a matchmaker for our kind, using her Fate hounds to seek out mates for humans blessed with divine blood. But it isn't beyond reason to think she'd do the same favor for one of us. And I am well aware of which primordial beings she has allied herself with who might ask for such a favor.

"Ssstop!" I bellow, and the sunlight darkens. The hounds yelp and blink away. The reverberating footsteps halt for a second, then keep coming.

I grit my teeth. "I do not permit godsss to enter without an invitation! You are tresspassssing!"

He has the audacity to laugh, his deep voice reverberating off the stone, working its way up every single one of my tails and settling deep in my belly. It only makes me angrier.

"Do you really want to risssk it?" I challenge. "You may not enter my aura without being ssstripped bare. If you come to me, you come as your true ssself and you sssurrender to my whim. Thisss is *my* domain."

I send my aura out in a pulsing wave down the open shaft visitors must climb to reach me. He will get a taste of what it feels like to lose purchase on his control.

"That tickles, my sibilant beauty. But I am more than just a god. Your rules do not apply to me."

The water around me vibrates, heating more the closer my visitor comes. I fix my gaze on the exit to the corridor. I sense him far down the shaft, but can't see him yet. His power dwarfs my own, and I push back, forcing with all my might to cool the water and hold his wild darkness at bay.

Only one creature in existence could overpower me to this degree. Despite fighting this unexpected invasion, part of me is curious what he will do when he arrives.

"Come if you mussst! But do not arrive cloaked in liesss. I want to sssee you in your esssence. You are entering *my* lair, therefore you will honor my rulesss."

"This is not an invasion, my sweet," he says. "This is courtship. Did you not see the hounds? We are meant to be, you and I."

"By whossse authority?" I scoff. "Fate hasss no dominion here."

"By mine. I require a mate who can match me in power. You, my dear, are quite perfect. I asked Ms. Rainsong to find me a mate, and she has more than delivered."

My nostrils flare. It's exactly as I suspected; Deva Rainsong's little pack of Fate hounds brought him here. It seems even without Fate asserting itself, its magic still led a horny primordial to my doorstep.

His deep chuckle echoes. "I take by your silence that you have grasped the situation. You know who I am."

"That doesn't mean I'll sssurrender easssily."

"Who says this has to be a fight? We are equals,

no? If you surrender to me, I will feed you so much power you can break free of this realm and go where you wish."

I snort. "You think I haven't been offered the sssame before? I have no wish to leave. I already have more power here than I need."

"Try me," he says, finally appearing in the opening of the corridor. Despite the narrow space available, he doesn't stoop; rather, the passage seems to swell to accommodate his immense size. It's as if the laws of physics are malleable within his aura.

Why I expected a man to appear, I don't know, but that is not what finally steps into my grotto.

He is an enormous half-bull, half-man with skin as black as night. His cloven hooves split the stone with every step, his horns nearly scraping the ceiling. Only one horn has a point, the other a jagged, broken tip. His muscles ripple, veins popping and writhing beneath his skin like snakes.

But his eyes are what give away his nature. The second he fixes them on me, I am unable to look away. All the secrets in the universe roil within those eternal depths, depths that are completely open to me despite his ability to keep me out. The power there is infinitely greater than that which was offered by the last pathetic creature who claimed they could set me free.

What Chaos offers is the key to existence itself.

His snout twitches, a smirk curling the edge of

his mouth. "You see what we can create if we work together? Will you birth a universe with me, my sweet Diviner?"

The sensation that overtakes me then is entirely foreign, but not unpleasant. I won't deny I derive some pleasure from the fun I have with the penitents who visit me, but this is the first time I've ever wanted to *be* violated. What he suggests is something I never considered: becoming the vessel for another creature's seed.

But what he offers in exchange is more than I could have ever imagined.

That's when I truly take him in, from the tip of his mismatched horns all the way down to his polished black hooves. Whorls of iridescent tattoos undulate up and down his arms, and over his chest. He has rings through both nipples that gleam in the now-returned sunlight, reflecting off the gems that line my walls. It's a wild kaleidoscope of color and light in here now, completely betraying my interest in his offer.

But I find I don't care when my eyes land on his cock, an appendage that may just be my utter destruction. The veins beneath its taut, black skin slither and twitch, and every tendril atop my head twists in interest.

He holds my gaze as he strides forward. Upon his first step into my pool, he sinks to his ankle, then his knee as he moves deeper, but the water never clears mid-thigh as he approaches, and his stiff cock and balls remain dry. The sheer scale of him dwarfs me by a full head—me, a creature twice the size of the largest satyr, and greater in proportion than any of my own half-siblings, the creatures who rule the higher races.

I'm used to being the biggest creature in the room, but when he closes in, the air leaves my lungs as I stare up at him, enthralled though hating myself just a little for how overcome I am by his presence.

His scent is wild, untamed, and he exudes his desire for creation from every pore.

"How can thisss work?" I ask. "You are *Chaosss*."

"I am the seed of all that is," he murmurs, lifting a hand to touch my cheek. "And you are the perfect vessel to receive me. Open for me, my flower."

The snakes streaming from my scalp snap at his fingers. He lifts one hand and holds it out, letting their tiny tongues taste his skin. His flavor seeps into me, lulling them as several coil around the end of his index finger.

I'm both hungry and frightened—hungry to absorb whatever power I could wrench from his body, if I could convince him to surrender to me, and frightened that I might be the one surrendering to *him*. If anyone could make me do it, he could. But I don't want to give in so easily.

I push two tails through the water between us, snaking them along the floor of the pool to ensnare his ankles. He glances down just as I begin sliding the tips up his thick legs. I take advantage of the brief distraction to whip four more tails around his wrists and upper arms. I pull, but he resists, as solid as the cave walls surrounding us.

But since he doesn't actually object, I keep going, forcing his arms behind him while I continue teasing my way up his legs. He may be hewn from solid muscle, but the softness of his balls are a vulnerability he didn't bother concealing.

"You did come to me in your true form. For that, I suppose I should give you credit." I wind one tendril around his heavy sac and the other around the base of his shaft. He merely watches me. I finally get a rise out of him when I venture between his ass cheeks with another tail-tip and tickle his anus. He bares his teeth and huffs a gout of steam from both big nostrils. His cock flexes in my grasp.

"Is this what you need? To see me undone? If it will make you trust me, then do your worst. You are the only creature in the universe who I would take as my mate. Only you can defy Fate so thoroughly. Join me, Sybil. Be my bride."

A surprised breath escapes me at the name he just gave me. I have only ever been one thing for my entire life: the Diviner.

Using my many tails, I lift myself to eye-level, hovering close with my hands on his shoulders. "Sssybil? Is that what I look like to you?"

He regards me with amusement. He knows he has me, but I also have him. He can't move his arms, and I'm keeping his cock in a punishing grip, barely teasing the tip while I slowly work one tail deeper into his ass.

He lets out a groan when I find the bundle of nerves inside him. So he isn't so different from other males, after all.

"You can be anything you wish at my side, my love. If you wish to be Sybil, I will make that happen."

"But only if I agree to let you *breed* me."

"That was an offer, not a condition. If you're unsatisfied with me today, then I will leave and never return."

I begin to stroke him faster, watching his reactions. Our gazes never waver, though his breathing quickens. I want to taste his power when he comes before I decide how far I am willing to go. I want to feel him surrender to me completely. Because in that moment of release, within their very essence, every truth about a creature is revealed.

It's a testament to his determination and strength that he remains standing while I torment him. I snake my tails around his entire body, touching every inch, from the tips of his horns to the clefts in his hooves, all the while stroking and fucking. Soon he releases a grunt, then a groan that builds into a bellowing roar so potent it nearly pushes me to climax, though he has yet to touch me beyond that first brush of his finger along my cheekbone. His shaft pulses and erupts into a long, brilliant stream of semen as iridescent as the marks upon his skin. It splashes against my scales, most of it falling into the water.

The second it lands, I gasp. My vision expands exponentially, as if I've only been looking through a tiny keyhole all this time and the door it's in was just blown wide. I sense *worlds* outside my lair that I had previously only gathered fragments of from my connection to the water that flows between them. But more than that, I see the sheer potential in what he just released, the futures that are possible if we share each other—if I give him my womb within which to grow a new universe for us to rule together.

I'm so dizzy with the possibilities, I release my hold on him entirely. I'd have fallen into the water, if not for his arms whipping back around to hold me up. I grab hold once more, coiling all my tails around his back and legs and staring at him in wonder.

"You would share all that with me?" I ask.

"Only you."

"Then make me yours however you see fit. I just have one request."

"Anything you wish."

"Show me your human face. I wish to kiss you. I wish to observe a proper nymphaea mating ritual and meld by tasting each of your three essences—saliva, semen, and blood. Will you do this for me?"

"If I have your leave to change, I will become whatever you wish."

I smile, baring my sharpened teeth. "Only your face for now, dear one. I like the rest of you as you are, but you lack lips for proper kissing."

He rumbles a laugh as his face transforms, the bull's snout receding until it's a somewhat asymmetrical, yet handsome human face. His dark skin and horns remain, as do the bull's ears and thick neck. I lift a hand and caress his jaw, still lost within that infinite gaze.

Curling my fingers around the back of his neck, I pull him in, heart pounding because kissing is not something I do. It's far too intimate and vulnerable an act, not to mention I have sharp teeth that could damage any of the penitents who visit.

Chaos doesn't flinch or hesitate. He captures my mouth hungrily when I press my lips to his, and drives his tongue deep into my mouth, heedless of the danger. I almost expect to taste blood before his saliva, but of course he's much too powerful to break so easily.

I am the one who breaks when the first taste of his essence hits my tongue. Despite the fact I am only sampling the weakest trace of his power, it leaves me privy to his surface thoughts.

He is consumed by nothing but pure desire—

desire for *me*. I push my own desires through that tenuous bond, and he responds instantly, tightening his hold around my waist as he strides through my pool to the shadows beyond, where my mossy bed is hidden. I don't want to release him, but he takes care when he puts me down to patiently remove each and every grasping tail from his body.

"Open for me," he says, caressing one hand up one of my frontmost tails.

My body quivers and my core throbs. This is a part of myself I *never* reveal to penitents... or anyone.

Swallowing harshly I separate my tails, twining them into two bundles that spread wide like legs. My core opens and my breathing quickens under his scrutiny.

He cocks his head and reaches out, mesmerized by what he sees. My flesh pulses as his hand approaches, and then he lightly flicks the swollen nub of my clit with the tip of his finger. "How many males have had the pleasure of seeing you this way?"

I want to lie, but find I can't. "I think you know the answer already."

"Mmm," he says, leaning over me and fully cupping my aching pussy. He digs his palm against my clit as he drops his mouth to my ear, ignoring the writhing tendrils and snapping teeth of my hair. "It will be my honor to show you what you are made for. Because it is a crying shame that this perfect pussy hasn't been pleasured the way it ought to have been.

Your melding requires an exchange, does it not? Then let me taste your essence first."

He falls to his knees before me, and I can't believe my luck. Chaos is *bowing* to me. Not only that, but he's pressing his lips to my cunt and burying his tongue deep inside.

I grab his horns and hold on tight, my tails losing control and whipping around him like dozens of wild vines. Some wrap around his head, holding him tight, while others slide down his torso on both sides, resuming their earlier torture. His cock is still hard and long, and cants to the side, his dark, bulbous head weeping more of that magical essence. I tease the tip of one tail through its flow, then raise it to my mouth, sucking the potent fluid off. With his tongue absorbing my own essence, a secret window flies open between our minds.

Eternity lies before me within the depths of his every thought, an eternity he wishes to share with me. He growls against my flesh, tongue lashing my clit faster and faster, his big fingers gripping the two closest tails to keep me spread wide. For the first time in my entire existence, I surrender to an urge I never thought I'd have.

I *change* for him.

Shifting is a skill I've always possessed, but have never used until now. I shrink until he towers over me, and he pulls away to watch in fascination as my many tails cling together and merge into two legs, my torso smooths into milky skin, and even the hair atop my head tames itself into red, silken strands that cascade over my shoulders and breasts.

Chaos pulls back more, studying my face, but keeping a thumb pressed to my clit to rub lightly. "You did not have to change for me. You are beautiful in your true form. A true goddess."

"I did this for me. I want to see myself through your eyes when you dominate me. Call it a fetish, a kink—a dirty fantasy I never thought I'd see fulfilled."

"You get off on the idea of fucking yourself?"

"No. I get off on the idea of being a creature strong enough to overpower someone like me. Let me into your head while you fuck me. Let me feel what it's like to be you."

"What it is like to be me is what it is like to be all things, precious Sybil. You think this is really my true form? What I *am* would not fit within the confines of this quaint little cavern. If you wish a taste, I will grant it to you, but first I will have you at my mercy."

He slides his hands up my thighs, and as he does, he changes yet again. His human-like face transforms, eyes growing, mouth widening. Hair sprouts from his chin, but it isn't really hair at all; it's a mass of tentacles not unlike my own natural locks, growing longer and thicker before my eyes.

Then he shoves my legs wide and descends

between them again, latching that monstrously beautiful orifice over my cunt once more. A tongue longer, thicker, and more agile than the one before drives deep enough to make me gasp, while the tentacles that surround his mouth tease and invade every other sensitive part of me until I'm screaming with the pleasure.

I've barely come down enough to refocus on the creature he has become. He's part bull, part nightmare, a creature of pure darkness. He coils his fleshy tendrils around me as he rises, his cock even bigger, its skin shining iridescent with escaped fluid.

I instinctively fight, but my struggles are fruitless. Through our link I grasp that *this* new shape is closest to his true form, and one of the reasons why he was so drawn to me to begin with.

Within the midst of that thought, I hear one clear message: "We are the same. Watch from behind my eyes if you wish, but don't forget to enjoy what it's like to be you, precious."

With that, he lifts me and holds my legs wide as he drives my transformed body down onto his waiting cock. I'm helpless to do anything but let it happen, a mere toy for this monster's pleasure. My pussy spreads as he plunges in, this tiny shape I took not nearly enough to accommodate something so large. I'm forced to adapt, to make room, because at this size, I can practically feel the tip of his cock at the back of my throat, despite being penetrated from below. Every inch of my insides experiences the thick, pulsing friction of his enormous shaft as he fucks me, and every slick cell of skin and muscle and organs *feels* it. My entire being is one big erogenous zone, and I completely surrender, obeying his command to enjoy myself while he treats me like his own personal Fleshlight.

My surrender is the trigger he needs to fully let go. With resonant grunts and bellows, he grows ever larger, more tentacles ripping from his sides. His arms and cloven hooves remain, but the obsidian orbs of his eyes multiply until there are dozens covering his head.

His tongue lashes across my breasts and down my belly to tickle my clit. I twist and squirm to no avail as another climax barrels through me. His deep chuckle is punctuated by the slurping slap of my helpless body on his enormous cock.

Then he roars as my muscles clamp down in the midst of my undoing. His semen floods forth, my core gripping and milking him for all he's worth. His seed fills me, overflowing in cascades that coat my legs and drip into the pool beneath us. My magic is still connected to the water, and I absorb every last ounce of power his come provides.

An infinity of magical essence floods my body, snapping me out of my haze of pleasure. It's *my* turn now.

I transform once more, my legs stretching and

splitting into dozens of tails again, and I grab hold of him, sinking all the way down his shaft, now that I can take him. He growls and tries to hold me fast, but not even his multi-tendril grip can resist my shifting form. With the surge of power, I grow even larger than I was before, my tails multiplying. He held my arms and legs before but can't keep up with the multitude of thrashing appendages. I clamp my body around his, gripping his cock tight within my hot sheath and squeezing rhythmically.

He lets out an unholy groan when one tail again finds its way to his ass and plunges in. His concentration falters and he stumbles back, giving me the upper hand. He falls, splashing into my pool with me on top. I hover over him, face close to his, and find his mouth amid all those twisting, writhing tendrils and blinking eyes. Our tongues twine and dance before we clamp together in a beastly kiss.

His tentacles roam my body slower now and I begin to move, rocking atop his cock at my own sweet, slow pace. I moan when one of his tentacles breaches my rear and others tease along my spine. Half a dozen grope around my head and neck, my serpentine hair snapping at his skin.

Tapered tips find every opening in my face, filling my nostrils and ears. The magic I've absorbed has heightened every one of my senses, making every penetration feel like I'm being fucked, and I give in kind. Soon we are nothing but a writhing mass of tangled tails and tentacles, his cock driving deep inside me with frantic thrusts, and we surrender to a shared climax that leaves us a quivering mess.

His flood of semen seeps from me, floating to the top of the pool like an oil slick and soaking into my skin. I've tasted him twice so far, but there is one last meld to share before we would truly be mates in the eyes of the Haven, the place I've called home for millennia.

I find my breath and graze his ear with my lips. "I wish to tassste your blood now. Will you take mine asss well?"

His face has softened and shifted back to features that are somewhat human, though he still has an extra eye or three. He nuzzles my breast and nods. "Take whatever you wish from me, precious Sybil. I give myself freely."

My mouth waters at his willingness, something that is rare among my penitents, though I find a bit of resistance from them makes things more exciting. But he is more than just a penitent; he is my mate.

I tease my forked tongue around the shell of his ear and down his thick neck, tasting, testing for a tender spot, but he turns his head and captures my mouth before I can bite. I whimper at the demand in his kiss, then feel sharp teeth digging into my lower lip. My body floods with fresh heat and desire when I catch on. His half-hard cock stiffens to steel again within my core, and I bite down on his lip in turn.

Blood floods our mouths, his and mine merging into one delicious cocktail of immense primordial power. He twists beneath me, flipping me to my back, though his tentacles keep me aloft as he drives his cock into me once more, thrusting over and over, all hard flesh and power.

We are one now in body, mind, and soul. His power is mine, and mine is his.

We remain joined for days, the earth around my grotto shaking with every climax we share. I never thought—never dared to hope—that a creature existed who could satisfy my needs so thoroughly. Chaos strips me down to my essence, forcing my surrender, then surrenders himself to my whims in return.

We are pure power in the end, and I can already feel the seed of a world taking root within me—a new universe birthed from power beyond anyone's wildest dreams.

MORE FROM OPHELIA

We hope you enjoyed ***Dominating the Demigoddess*** by Ophelia Bell!

If you're curious about the Diviner and the roles she and Chaos play in their world, immerse yourself in Ophelia's *"Immortal Dragons"* series.

These six immortal dragons are the lawmakers of their kind, but they aren't immune to Fate's edicts any more than the rest of their race. When Fate sends them prophetic dreams of the mates they are meant for, they know better than to ignore the call.

Ophelia Bell writes sexy dragon shifters and other magical races in her menage and reverse harem stories, all of which feature epically endowed heroes.

WWW.OPHELIABELL.COM

IN THE BURN GARDEN

BY ISOELLEN

IN THE BURN GARDEN

ISOELLEN

The sun heated Binda's head and back until she couldn't take another moment of it. Dragging her hoe behind her, she sought the shade of the orchard. There was always a restless little wind waiting for her under the knotted limbs of the old cherry tree.

If anyone knew Binda's vegetables and fruit came from this forbidden bit of land, they'd never eat another thing she brought to barter. Good lord above and below, it was just soil and sky with a bit of weirdness thrown in. And after the Fall, most places and people had at least a little weirdness attached to them. When it came to eating and profit, Binda had no time for town superstition. What they didn't know wouldn't hurt them.

The moment she sat under her favorite tree, she pulled her lunch bag into her lap, and lifted the hair off her neck. She felt that blessed air. They'd made friends, they had. Little tendrils of it played over her cheeks, the sweat on her brow, and down her front. She laughed at the fancy thought that the wind was as gentle as a lover's fingers. Not that she knew too much about that.

Undoing the string she'd used to replace the buttons on her top, she opened her shirt. Beneath was a make-shift bra and back support system she created herself, a side-laced get-up of salvaged bands and straps. Life as a gardener was hard work. Doing it all on her own gave new meaning to the word back-breaking.

The air felt so good on her neck that she released the straps of her bra, shucked her boots, stockings, pantaloons, and gathered her skirt up to her waist. Half-naked and exposed, Binda cooled quickly.

Wouldn't all the married ladies of Main Street have a fit if they saw her now? But they wouldn't. Not here. And that, really, was the whole point.

At the height of the burn season, the sun forced Binda to take her breaks in the middle of the day—the heat was just too much. She'd learned two years ago that in spring and fall she could work on through the afternoon, but she'd pass out if she kept going during this time of year.

Her sack held the light lunch of a poor woman—a jar of last year's strawberry jam, bread, hard cheese, and black bean crackers. There was half a skin of water and a full bottle of her own brand of bad homemade wine.

It was quiet here. Chewing the crackers made a racket in her head. Birds and critters were as touchy about this out-of-the-way-place as people were. Did the energy here feel different, or were the birds as superstitious as the town in places where thousands of people burned to ash in clouds of white phosphorus?

Everyone said this was not a good place.

All those people who died in a single attack during the chaos of the Fall, turned to fertilizer, which plumped her pumpkins and tomatoes twice the size of anyone else's.

That horrific day left behind few heroes. But it wasn't the only history this place carried. There was more. Binda found things daily in the garden, lost things from ages past, with no business finding their way to sunlight. Bright enameled pottery, coins, buckles, and rusted metal, time-nibbled bits like the knife blades John Blacksmith crafted in town, piled against the trunk of another old tree nearby. The mound got bigger every day. The lack of ready-made goods now had returned the craft of shaping iron to popularity, but Binda should not be finding ancient look a-likes in her garden.

When Binda went to drink more water, the skin was empty. Meal finished, she grabbed the wine as lunch's finale. It would make her sleepy and a nap was not a bad idea. Wind tugged her hair free of the loose tie on top of her head and played with it, spreading it out over her shoulders. Her newest discovery from the garden winked at her in the dappled sun, asking for closer inspection. She discovered the undamaged green and black bottle under the leaves of her squash and cucumber plants that morning. The black scrolly designs around the neck and at the bottom looked like tarnished silver. John Blacksmith would barter free service on all her tools for silver like that.

Taking it in hand, she found the glass cold to the touch, a frigid chill against her fingertips. There was something inside, but liquid or dust, she couldn't say. The weight of it moved in a slow ooze as she turned the treasure. In less than a minute, her hands hurt too much from the odd cold, so she covered them with her skirt and used the material to clean away the dirt.

Expecting to find a rotting cork stopper or a waxed-over seal, Binda noted the lid clamped down with a lever of more black metal fine detail work. The caps at the top and bottom created singular whorls and scroll-like elaborate cursive handwriting. It also sported a line of four metal hoops. Did it once have a strap to wear the bottle over a shoulder? The odd lid looked as if it was also missing a piece. A lock, perhaps.

She'd never seen anything like it.

Fingering the lid, she must have tripped a switch,

because it popped open and made her jump. Binda would have laughed at her foolishness, but bright, ghastly red smoke and an exotic scent poured out of the thing.

She continued to hold the bottle for a second, in shock, inhaling smoke as it billowed out over her face and head. The smell wasn't unpleasant, but that red color meant nothing good. Binda tossed the bottle and crab walked backwards, crashing into the tree behind her.

Fight or flight lost out to awe as smoke continued to pour out of the bottle straight up into the air. Instead of dispersing, it bubbled into a nightmare creature. Head, shoulders, wings, and legs spread wide in aggression.

A too-big head and wide mane of black curls emerged first from the red smoke. Then a face appeared a snarling animal muzzle with massive canine teeth above a neck and shoulders thicker than that bull of a man John Blacksmith, the strongest man Binda knew. Dark colored skin stood out in sharp relief against the garish smoke, shades of ebony and onyx highlighted poisonous green against billowing red. The smoke stayed tight, sinking into the body it created. Wings appeared to go with the predator head, a muscled torso and, last, an upright, aroused cock.

"Lords above and below. Oh, hells no! It always comes to that with you males, doesn't it?" Binda twisted to escape the naked monster from the bottle. Now would be a good time to run, but the wind no longer teased her—it became her enemy.

Invisible air wrapped around her wrists and roped them over her head into the bark of the decrepit cherry tree. This was why people avoided places attached to stories of the weird and the tragic. But it was too late now.

"I know who I am. You have no power over me, monster," she shouted at the thing.

Her will was her greatest weapon. Binda was not fool enough to come garden in the bright burn like this without it.

The dense smoke continued to sink into the naked body of the male, surely some sort of inhuman creature from the time of the Fall. She lacked the education to name his type or origins. He looked like parts of things put together from an insane imagination. Standing very tall, he was too strange to be born in any natural way from the body of a woman, but still passionately elemental and fully, fiercely alive.

Stretching arms and wings open under the afternoon sky, he greeted Binda with a dramatic roar. The tree at her back trembled. Or maybe that was Binda.

It took four long-legged strides for him to tower over her. His cock stood out from his body, *right there*, waving a crude hello. She'd laugh at it if the male connected to it was even a smidge less frightening. An aroused cock always looked silly, but Binda held her tongue. The hard body of the male and his dangerous intensity left no air for humor. His erection looked painful and urgent, dark-night blue at the crown and bruised purple down to the thick base where male hair curled above the heavy pendulum of his testicles.

And a tail. *Of course* he had a tail. Snaking forward, it brushed the bare inseam of her foot in a curious touch. She should have jerked away. Fought. Something.

The wind was the betrayer who captured her today. Or was it his magic? Because fizzling magic saturated this beast-bottle-man, crackling between them.

Perhaps it was one of Binda's own needs keeping her bound up. Her need for touch. Her need to be known. Her need to never be afraid again. There were so many in a situation like this to pick and choose from.

The monster was a frightening, beautiful thing, eyeing her up and down like water on a hot day. Every muscular line of him was imbued with menace. He snapped sharp teeth at her. Or was that a smile?

Difficult to tell, but the shiver streaking through her chest felt like all her memories of fear. And she'd made vows not to walk away from that feeling, not if an opportunity to face it with her stupid belligerence presented itself.

Moments like this never ended in her favor. There'd be a price to pay, but she did it, anyway. "You have no power over me. You cannot take what I do not give."

His voice came out in a growl, some sounds odd because of the shape of his mouth. "And yet you cannot move, because of my command."

"But I freed you from your prison. Is this what you do to everyone who is nice to you?"

He cocked his head, his tail moving against her vulnerable skin, a stroke that tickled.

Binda knew how this worked. Names had power. She wanted his. "What is your name?"

He sneered at her.

Binda waited, heart pounding, and watched his eyes. He had all the strength in the situation, despite his nakedness. The smell of his spice inundated her senses. Was it doing something to her mind? Her self-control? It wasn't pepper, cumin, or chili, or anything she recognized. The delicious aroma snuck into her head and sank hot into her skin. Binda could lose herself to it. "What is your name? Tell me now. What is your name?"

His eyes roved over her, ignoring the question and reminding Binda of her open shirt and unfastened bra. He could see everything. On display, her nipples hardened, pointing at him in puffy, swollen invitation. Her pulse beat trapped-rabbit-fast at the base of her throat.

"Who are you? Where do you come from? What. Is. Your. Name?" she pressed.

"They call me Kore."

"That is not what I asked," she snapped.

"You get what I say."

"Tell me your name, Beastly-Bottle-Man." She used the taunt like a dart. This was important. Binda knew it.

His lip curled at what she had called him. "Valkore De Nuit."

"Valkore De Nuit." She repeated it out loud, three times, exactly. The sound moved from her lips and rippled down the bumps and curves of his body, making his cock jerk.

He smelled very good. He looked even better.

If John Blacksmith didn't have two wives and a hammy fist, Binda would have taken that man up on his last offer to exchange sex for iron. It had been so long since anyone touched her with interest or affection. Sometimes she wondered if she was still alive. Maybe she was just a ghost hovering over her vegetables. Rough and uncomfortable sex in the back of a smithy would remind her she was still a woman. Still here. As it was, this beast man was the healthiest, cleanest, most interested male she had yet to come across. And he was *very* interested.

He affected her, standing unashamed and staring her down. Her core grew damp from his concentrated interest. Was he waiting for the drug of his scent to take effect and steal her reason? He wouldn't wait long. Not this type of hunter. Unlike the burn of the noon-day sun, the heat of his regard sank past her skin into her being, sensitizing all her female parts.

He said, "You have freed me. Claim your reward. Wealth. Power or pleasure."

"There is a reward? Like what you get when you report law breakers to the Affinity Board? No thanks." She knew he didn't mean that. But that last word and his eye-level cock were playing havoc with her will and desires. Could she release one and not the other? Could she touch him and not lose her will to him?

"You have done me a good deed. I will reward you." She watched as he carefully licked his lips. His tongue stood out lewd pink against his night-colored skin, longer and more mobile than it had any right to be. It turned her mind back to that last offered reward.

Don't say it, Binda. But she did. *Of course* she did. "Pleasure? Are you a sex god, captured as a slave by some kind of vengeful hag who you refused to please?" There were stories of captured gods after the Fall. Kore was unusual enough in size and power to be one of them.

He smirked. "No. Say your reward."

"No, not a sex god? Not a god? No hag

involved?" She was trying to be funny and distance herself from that word. He didn't smile.

His brows lowered and the green of his eyes darkened to grave-stone ivy. "No."

He didn't like games and sass, then. She was in so much trouble. "I say my reward and then the wind will set me free, and you will, what? Be on your way, birth day naked, flag waving as you walk?"

In answer, his wings flapped, gusting the wind and pushing his scent in her face.

"Fly away, then. Not walk," Binda said.

The invisible rope of her former friendly wind pulled her legs apart wide enough for him to step between.

She should be more alarmed and less interested, but her heart was racing from the wrong motivations. His actions thrilled her. What was wrong with her? This was not a good or kind man. His colors were those of death. That bottle was a prison, meant to shame and punish. He had to be dangerous. To remind herself, and warn him, she said, "My soul is my own. I know who I am. Where I've been, where I've come from, and I damn-well know where I am going. You have no power over me that I do not give, Valkore De Nuit."

Despite her declaration, she couldn't close her legs against the invisible force.

He smiled at her predicament.

Willpower was a tricky thing, indeed.

The wind pulled her down, dragging her over the ground just enough to lay her on her back, keeping her arms pinned and legs wide, presenting her as an offering to the ugly-gorgeous man. He pounced, the intimidating male landing over her and caging her in his masculinity. Magic and sexual tension twisted in the space between their bodies, lashing Binda's skin.

"What is your name?" he asked, still only touching Binda with his tail.

"You can call me Queen."

The noise in his throat sounded like a chuckle. "I can? Queen. What are you? Human? Other? More?"

"Me. I'm me." He was too close, hovering over her like he was. Under a heavy brow, his emerald eyes glowed with hunger.

Snapping his wings open, he covered them both with twilight beneath his broad raptor's canopy. Binda saw a shimmer in the innermost feathers that matched his eyes, a hint of contrasting color tucked in the endless, unrelenting velvet and stone black. Her fingers twitched, wanting to touch. Wanting.

No. No. No. That wouldn't do.

Want and need were sneaky, vicious little imps lurking in corners behind emotions, corrupting rational thinking. Willpower could be as changeable as the wind now holding her. If her will changed, his power over her changed. Magic could not touch her as long as she rejected it. Nothing harmed her without her permission.

The threat of his closeness tempted instead of repelled. He wasn't human, but he was alive. Wildly, vitally alive. Years of emptiness bricked up the time between Binda and any kindness or attention from another person. Desire and loneliness rattled together inside her heart, wanting out, begging to be cracked open and spilled free. They wanted out of the prison where she had bottled them up and hidden them away.

Kore devoured her responses, holding Binda at the center of his attention. Whatever motivations he hid in his head, right now, he wanted to mate her and ease his hard, unsatisfied cock with her body. With *her*. From the first moment, his desire had slipped under Binda's defenses and self-preservation, seducing her.

"What is your command for me, Queen? What service can I give to you for freeing me? You seem a wise and careful thing. You know how this works then, yes? I cannot leave you until I reward you."

"What reward?" she asked.

"I am bound and must offer service. I want to. You have done me a good deed. Let me serve you, Queen. And now you have my name. You can do with me as you please. Whatever you want. What could that be?" Soothing her with soft touches, his tail climbed her calf.

Kore said the word service like a pre-attack vow. He might have said: *How would you like me to hunt you, my Queen? How would you like me to take your breath away and fuck you? How would you like me to own you, forever?*

Powerful and inhuman, Kore was no one's slave. He maintained the boldness and passion of a warrior. Binda was just a farmer who should tremble with fear, cower, and cry. For sure, a bit of reasonable anxiety would help her find the will to fight herself.

She just needed a little. Was that too much to expect? Just enough honest caution to knock some sense of reality into her. But to fear, she had to have something worth losing, and Binda couldn't think of a single damn thing more awful that *not* letting this man touch her. Everywhere. It would only be her third time having sex. This time, it could be good. Enhanced with the compelling drug of his unworldly magic, it had *better* be good.

"You offered pleasure. Then for the next hour, I want all the pleasure, everything I've never had. Give me pleasure for the next hour that the sun crosses the sky and no longer. Not a second longer. After an hour you will stop, Valkore De Nuit, and no longer have permission, neither you nor your magic, to touch any part of me."

His eyes widened and glittered. He said nothing about the latent binding in her sentences—pretended not to hear that part. Instead, he grumbled a response that felt like a promise in her ear, "An hour is not long enough."

"An hour," she insisted, choking out a gasp as his head dipped closer to her and his tail rose higher. He didn't hesitate. Lowering himself, he kissed her right between her breasts at the same time his tail discovered the junction of her thighs.

He purred at what he found, a complimenting sound that made Binda feel beautiful.

His tail discovered wet, willing woman, so swollen from the sight and smell of him that the petals of Binda's vulva parted, and her hardened clit peaked through, already begging for his touch.

"I see you now," he said against her skin. Licking her. "Queen. Poor lonely Queen. No suitor to honor you. Let me, a starved old warrior, lap at your cup. Let me honor you."

Brushing his muzzle back and forth, he swept his mouth against her skin, bringing him closer to her painfully untended nipples. His tail petted back and forth against her slit, rubbing her pleasure spot, but giving no pressure. Its tapered end fit just so. It felt too good. Much too good. Want built. He became the focus of all her energy. She couldn't help herself.

"All this white milky skin. An angel. Even the burn doesn't mark you, not a single freckle or spot. I do not think I can be so kind," he said against her skin with a nip of teeth, drawing blood.

"You want more than to honor me. You want

more than my pleasure," she moaned. If she could have coughed out a bittersweet laugh, she would have.

She guessed Kore a taker by nature. He'd twist the generosity of giving Binda pleasure upside down and swallow it all for his own satisfaction. Whatever Kore was, owning her would be his goal, because he was a creature who claimed and discarded. He didn't borrow, ask, or wait, and hated having to be granted the permission. But he'd captured her want. For the next hour, she was at his mercy.

Nuzzling his way around the curve of her breast, he engulfed her nipple with his mouth, sucking her in while his tail finally applied pressure in just the right place. He suckled with brutal hunger, pulling at her, his teeth digging in as that tail, like a third hand, rubbed at her peak with short little touches.

Binda struggled at the phantom bindings on her arms and tried to arch away from his mouth and up into the touch between her legs. He marked each breast, sucking her nipples red and stiff. Pointed teeth scraped along her sternum, making her skin come alive. He licked and feasted, teeth at her collarbone, then her neck. Lacking true lips, his tongue made up for any slight. He cooed, "Strong little queen in peasant clothes. Where are your silks and velvets? Where is your engraved armor? You have been so neglected."

His tail moved, moved, moved. His mouth stayed

gentle while the waves of delight built, folding over themselves again and again. Staying patient, giving her time, he kept his rhythm. He only touched her with his mouth, face, and tail. Instead of tickling, his whiskers stroked and reassured as he lapped at her neck, waiting.

Pressure built inside her until she was there, ready to come. Her pleasure froze when he sucked the soft flesh under her ear against the sharp points of his teeth.

She gasped at the dual shock of pain and pleasure.

Why? Who would find this pleasurable? This was torture. She didn't like the pain. It made her orgasm falter and stick. Kore had deliberately kept her from falling into bliss.

Frustrated, she hissed at him, would have spoken, but night enclosed her body as he turned them and sat her right over his cock. Glorious in repose, his wings spread open, onyx black skin that ate the day light. She rode the body of a fantasy creature, a male of thunder and lightning. She was small and feminine against his size and strength. His hands scraped away the remains of her clothing, baring everything before cupping her breasts, tugging and pinching her nipples in play.

Panting, she moved her hips. His cock speared her needy, pulsing seam. That tail of his stroked the line of her spine, spreading heat with a reckless hope.

"I have your reward. Will you take it?"

"I almost had it before. You ruined it." She wanted to sound queenly. Instead, her voice came out small and petulant. Damn him.

He laughed, a sound from his chest she felt in her pussy. "Put me inside you and we shall see if you are ruined or prepared."

Getting her feet under her weight, riding desire, Binda took the thick bar of his manhood in her hand, rubbing it against herself where she needed it, the same place he'd rubbed his tail.

Long and thick, his cock was bigger than the others she'd taken. It might hurt, filling her up. This was good. She could be satisfied with this.

His hips bucked, impatient. *He* was not satisfied at all. Insistently, he urged the silk of his cock faster. Back and forth in her hand, bumping the blunt head against her softness. The seductive spice of his scent filled the air, stealing her reasoning with the sultry smell. Back and forth, then a grunt, a thrust, his hands at her thighs opening her wider. Palms at her waist, claws scraped her back and set it on fire, then pulled her down without mercy—the head of his cock breaching her hole.

Binda sucked in a breath. He bucked again. So much of him. She held herself still, speared by his flesh.

Kore growled long and low with victory and appreciation. In answer, Binda's inner muscles quivered. Taking her reward, she spilled around him in exquisite surrender. Magic and power swirled in a thin cloud around them. Binda watched it shimmer at the edge of her vision, greening the abandoned cherry orchard. A dark threat of the unknown she suddenly had no will to stop.

He was in and she was full. In another dizzying move, he put Binda under him, scraped her bare back on the ground as he pulled her legs up, ramming deep with a hard slap of skin against skin. Her breasts jiggled with the movement, the tips raw and throbbing from his earlier attention.

"Oh, my Binda, you are as perfect as I knew you'd be," he said between grunts timed with his thrusts.

Binda whined her answer, too full to speak or think. It felt amazing and horrifying, a connection filled with menace. He'd said her name when he shouldn't know it. And she didn't care. She didn't care about anything but getting more.

Just don't stop. Don't stop. His hips moved, knocking her back. He handled her roughly, with more growls. She wanted to cry out in pain, but his taking burned inside her, starting a fire that heated her all over. As he leaned down, she realized he was too long in the torso for her to even reach his neck or face with her mouth, but his chest was there. Hands finally free, she wrapped herself around him, into him, opened her mouth and tasted the darkness.

Spice singed her tongue, smoked her taste buds, made her mouth water for more.

Don't stop. More.

Hips thrusting, he gave her the pounding of her life. They squelched together with noisy and profane combined wetness. United together in a release of their unwilling abstinence and isolation. This was a male born for killing and fucking. And it had been a long time for them both.

His pumping jostled her emotions as much as her body, knocked at doors fastened down tight, rattling her inner locks until tears surged behind her eyes. Binda moaned low, feeling the hinges of her hidden-self shake as screws came loose. Her mind opened, will unfurling under the pressure of his cock rubbing at her inner secrets.

He felt good there. Right. But it was too much.

She howled in denial. Too close, and much too dear. But Binda could no more push him away than she could ask him to stop.

Then he leaned forward, lifted her up on top of his thighs, wrapped his arms around her, and brought her close to his chest and under his chin. Off the ground and in his lap, Kore held Binda together in the binding of his arms as he sank deeper into her body and being. Wings spread for balance, his mane of hair became a halo. She was sure a god of myth filled her woman's center.

The new position pressed her clit against a

roughened bulge above his cock. Hidden by the thick of pubic hair, she hadn't noticed it until just now, centered in the perfect spot for her to press herself. And she did, with choppy moans and squeals. His hands and hips bounced her against him again and again. With Binda's ass off his lap and her thighs opened completely to him, Korc's tail found her exposed pucker and tapped.

Sensation overwhelmed her, took her to the edge again. Her peak rose swiftly. It felt huge, able to crack her open and fill her up with fire.

Beating his wings, air whooshed around them while his pelvis moved with short humps, those muscled arms pulling her down while he thrust up. Mouth at her neck, his tongue stroked in circles. He held her so tight she couldn't move her arms, his strength and size leaving her helpless.

Binda failed to lock her legs around him, rubbing herself urgent and desperate against his hidden nodule of flesh, her womb squeezing tighter and tighter as his cock thickened. She could only take what he gave, accepting waves of pleasure as they built. Refolded, reshaped right to the precipice, where she tipped over the edge with a scream and went up in fire.

Her inner door burst open under the explosion, the locks disintegrating. The rush was feral. His manhood grew until she couldn't move, her center gripping him tight enough to feel the dull pulse of his answering release under the potent frenzy of her own undoing.

The male's seed burned. Filling her up. The lava flowed into the cavity of her pussy and pooled into her hips, spreading through her torso and heading toward her mind. She shuddered with the shock of the invasion, her leg kicking out, her foot hitting the cold of Kore's former bottle prison.

The cold pulled her out of their intimacy and back into reality.

"Binda Mine," he said against her neck, opening his mouth, his teeth breaking skin.

"No. No. I am my own. Your hour is up. Go back in your bottle. You will not take my will."

He stiffened with rage. Stuck in his embrace, Binda screamed as his arms squeezed. Wings beating in a storm, his hands opened on her back. His claws tore into Binda's exposed skin, trying to anchor his shape to this world. But her command controlled him, forcing the transformation from black into green, to dark blue, to purple and finally red smoke.

Binda dropped to the ground with a teeth-snapping grunt, leaking pleasure and semen from between her legs and bleeding from her wounded back. Scrapes from his teeth burned on her neck and shoulders. Kore hadn't time to yell or argue, so quick was his return to the prison of his bottle.

No one would take what she did not give. Not ever again. Nothing could tempt her. *Nothing*. Not a male with an incredible body. Not the promise of respite from loneliness. Not momentary pleasure.

She was Binda, gardener of the Burn, and her soul was her own. She knew where she came from and where she was going.

For now, there was no wind at all. No birds. No sound but Binda's heartbeat and panting breaths. The bottle, with Kore locked inside, sat beside her. There were loops attached to the blackened metal.

She would need a strap.

MORE FROM ISOELLEN

We hope you enjoyed ***In The Burn Garden,*** by Isoellen!

Continue reading works by Isoellen in the *Orki War Bride* Series.

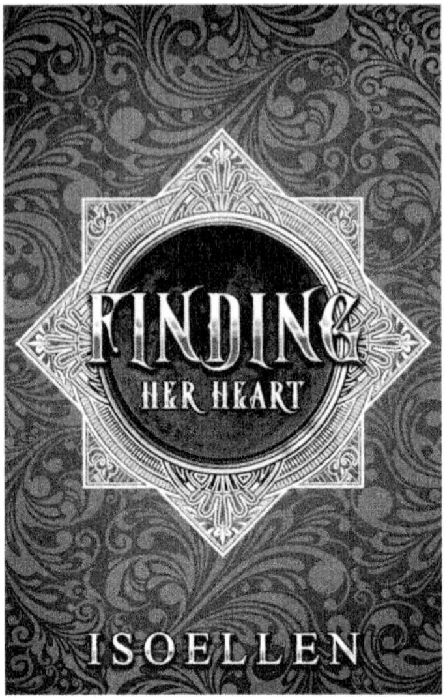

It is said there is only one woman for every Orki warrior
If she is born far from his grasp, chooses another, or dies, he will never know the warmth of her comfort. For she is the only one for him. His redress woman. His reward. No other woman can know him, see him, love him

---

Isoellen writes omegaverse and other worldly romance set in sex drenched, violent worlds. Vist her on social media. She is the only Isoellen and loves to talk to readers.

WWW.ISOELLEN.COM

STAR CROSSED

BY LESLIE CHASE

STAR CROSSED

LESLIE CHASE

In hindsight, drinking coffee during the transition out of hyperspace was a terrible idea, but how was I to know? I'd done this a thousand times, and every one of them I'd dropped into realspace to see black emptiness punctuated with distant stars.

This time a chunk of starship hull the size of a car greeted me. I barely had time to swerve out of its path, and it wasn't alone.

The sensors filled with vectors showing dozens of contacts, all whirling in different orbits. I dodged the second piece to come my way, but the third hit, and hit hard. Luckily for me, it was small enough not to tear my ship in half. That was the only good news.

The *Stardancer* jerked and shook from the impact, artificial gravity failing for a second. I had just enough time to see the coffee float free of its cup, a weird dark sphere, before the gravity snapped back on. The hot coffee went from floating to splashing instantly. On me, on the controls, on the photo of my family I kept on the wall for good luck. *Everywhere.*

Behind me, in the living area, Freefall yowled a protest. As the ship's cat, she had every right to complain, but as the ship's human, I ignored her. With the holoprojectors covered in coffee the displays were unreadable chaos and I ran through every swearword I knew in English, Galtrade, Spanish, and Hormza as I tried to steer onto a safe course from memory. If the coffee got into the circuits and fried them, there was no repairing them, but if another of those hunks of junk hit I'd be just as dead.

Alarms blared all around me, overlapping each other as I settled into what I thought was a junk-free orbit. "Yes, I know," I called back to the cat, pulling off my stained t-shirt and using it to mop up the spill as fast as possible. No way was I about to leave the pilot's chair to look for a more suitable cloth, not when every second counted.

The displays blurred back into visibility as I scrubbed the projectors. Too many of them were red for my liking, but the most pressing was the proximity alarm, flashing COLLISION IMMINENT in unmissable urgency. I grabbed the controls, abandoning clean up in favor of survival and cursing the universe for not giving me a moment to catch my breath.

"What the *fuck*—" I stared at the sensor display,

incredulous. Dozens had been an understatement—there were hundreds of contacts. No, thousands, moving in different directions at various speeds. Instead of arriving at the edge of the debris field as I'd intended, I'd landed in the middle of it. My shock lasted a second too long, and the clang of something hitting the hull rattled my bones.

The lights flickered and a horrible grinding noise behind me filled my heart with dread. If the impact tore the ship open, that would be that.

No deadly whistle of escaping air followed, though, and the lighting steadied. I got my breathing under control as I maneuvered the *Stardancer* out of the way of more incoming debris. The scanners picked up more details on the near-misses, and I whistled, my eyes widening. Rumors of an Elder Race wreck had led me here, but I'd never expected this much treasure to be flying around. This was the richest I'd ever seen, enough to start a gold rush, and I was here first. At the heart of the debris was the big prize, a battleship nearly a kilometer long, untouched in the ten thousand years since the Elder War.

If I could get to it, filling the *Stardancer's* hold with salvage would make for the biggest payday Stardancer Salvage had seen since Grandma founded the firm.

Unfortunately, big prizes made for big junkfields. I'd expected a much smaller vessel, a destroyer at most. No one expected to find a battleship, it was like hitting a dozen jackpots at once. Over the millennia, scavengers had picked the big battlefields clean. Somehow, this one went unseen until a couple of astronomy undergrads on the closest planet spotted the faint traces of the Elder gravitic engines, and rumors started to spread.

A smaller wreck and my jump would have put me far enough out to assess the salvage safely, while still being close enough to get in fast before some of the bigger players turned up and claimed everything. Instead, I'd landed in the middle of this whirling vortex of junk.

"At least now I can see where's safe," I said to Freefall as I shunted the *Stardancer* into a path with relatively few chunks of spaceship to avoid. In this chaotic swarm of wreckage, safety was a fragile and temporary thing, but now I could afford to split my attention. "We're alive, the *Stardancer's* still flying, and the wreck is much bigger than I thought. I've even beaten Kyross here. This is a good day."

Freefall tilted her head to the side and flicked her ears. I didn't blame her for her skepticism—I had to get enough salvage to pay for the repairs as well as turn a profit.

"Time to see how much trouble I'm in," I said. The collision alarm had stopped screaming at me, so I could spare the attention to see how fucked I was. "Status report."

The damage control display glowed an ominous

red, and reports scrolled past. I greeted each one with a different swearword.

Life support: marginal. Fuck. Survivable, but frightening. The ship was rated for six adult humans, so Freefall and I would be fine unless things deteriorated, but it would be an expensive repair.

Communications: short range only. Damn. The impact had sheared off the long-range antenna. I didn't want to call for help, but the option would have been nice. I kept the short-range retracted and safe—the antenna would give me a longer range, but that wasn't worth the risk of losing it.

Engines: 73% function. Shit. That looked worse than it was: I'd launched with them at 80%. Couldn't afford to put any more stress on them, though.

Hyperdrive: offline.

"Fuck*shit*goddamn."

That was the most coherent thought I could form. Without a hyperdrive, my chances of surviving this little disaster dropped from 'slim' to 'laughable.' Like most leftovers from the War, this debris field lay well away from inhabited space, far enough out that the sun it orbited just looked like a brighter-than-usual star. With a hyperdrive, home was a week away. In realspace, just getting back to the inhabited inner system would take months.

"Assuming the engines hold," I muttered. "And the food stock lasts. And—"

The collision alarm blared again, loud enough to

drown out my thoughts. This time I was ready and before I thought about it, I'd jinked the *Stardancer* out of the way of a chunk of hull nearly as big as my ship. The yowl of a cat being rudely flung about by my desperate maneuvers replaced the alarm.

"Sorry, sorry," I called back without looking. Freefall could fend for herself on a spaceship, and I needed my attention on the scanners and thrust controls. Debris floated everywhere, and the prize I planned to loot lay right at the heart of it.

Backing out might have been the smart plan, but I had no intention of coming home with a half-wrecked ship and an empty hold, ruining the family business. Second best would be to fly clear of the debris, get some distance and look for things worth snatching from the edges of the vortex. But that would take time, and time I didn't have. The one advantage of being a small business was that we could respond to news fast.

The wreck of an Elder battleship would get all our rivals scrambling for a share. The longer I took to stake my claim on the valuables, the more risk that one of the big players would turn up and keep me away from the good stuff. They might be slower getting here, but once they arrived, I wouldn't be able to keep up. Even another small firm would be competition I didn't need.

"So, stupid plan it is." Realigning the *Stardancer,* I aimed for the center of the debris and pushed the thrusters, easing my way in past whirling junk. There was treasure out there, too, but on my own I couldn't get to it. Too much danger of the *Stardancer* taking a hit while I was trying to wrangle something into the hold. I needed to be safe in the eye of the storm.

It took too long, and there were too many close calls, but eventually I found my way through to the torn-open hull of the Elder battleship. Some ancient weapon had left a hole large enough to fit a ship into, and under that protection, I could risk getting out and scavenging. There was only one problem.

The hiding place was already taken.

Another modern ship was wedged into the tangle of broken struts, and I had to admit that was an impressive bit of flying. I hated to admit that, because I knew that ship and who it belonged to.

The Kyross Collective. Our nemesis, the other big fish in the small pond of independent salvage. Also a family concern, one we'd been feuding with for generations, and the reason I was alone on this trip. Stardancer Salvage used to be a family business, and maybe it would be again someday. Right now, though, the two of us were the only active crew. Dad got his license suspended after an 'accidental' collision with a Kyross Collective's ship. Mom was too busy managing the business to ship out, and she needed my brothers around for security. Gemma, my sister, had a broken leg after her run in with the

Kyross, which is what got dad mad enough to clip their ship.

There ought to be cousins around too, but all of them found other work as the feud between us and the Kyross heated up. I couldn't say I blamed them. The constant conflict wasn't just dangerous, it kept the business on the brink of bankruptcy. If this weren't my family firm, I'd have joined them.

And now, the Kyross Collective was blocking my access to the battleship's riches. To the salvage I needed to keep my family afloat. I drummed my fingers on the control console, counting back from ten and trying to relax my shoulders. By the time I reached zero, I felt a little calmer.

"Okay, Freefall, I can't fit in that gap with them, and I can't see any other way in. I think I'm going to have to talk to them and see if we can work out a deal. Maybe they'll give me a lift home?"

Freefall hissed at that, and I agreed with her. My plan sounded naïve, but what choice did I have? The Kyross might help me for bragging rights, a big corporation would claim my ship as salvage for certain. If there was even a chance of getting the *Stardancer* back to Hudson Station, I had to take it.

After a final check for incoming debris, making sure I was safe for the next few minutes, I extended the antenna. Mouth dry, one eye on the collision detector, I scanned for signals again. It was a risk, leaving the vulnerable antenna out where the slightest impact could sever it. But what use was it if I didn't use it?

The ship, identifying itself as the *Third Sunrise*, was already broadcasting at me. With gritted teeth, I switched on the comms.

"... my salvage. Back off." The first words made out through the static were harsh, and the scowling alien face wasn't much friendlier. A rugged face, with a scar running from his forehead down to his cheek, interrupted by a metal eye replacement. His other eye, dark and brooding, stared at me from the screen. He made an arresting sight—blue skin, a deep blue like lapis lazuli, and in place of hair, thick quills pulled back from his face, shimmering in the emergency lighting. Horns rose through them, an eerie white against the darker blues.

He looked like a space pirate out of a holonovella, the 'bad guy' that everyone secretly wished would carry off the heroine.

It took me a moment to recognize him. Krell Kyros had grown up since I'd last seen him, years ago. Our families might be feuding, but we couldn't avoid each other completely. We hadn't spoken beyond an awkward introduction, and I'd only seen him a few times. It wasn't easy to reconcile the sullen youth of my memories with the man I saw in the hologram. Strong, confident, rugged—the perfect villain to drag me back to his asteroid lair.

Izzy! What the hell? Maybe being out here in the

dark with no company was wearing on me, if that was my first thought when a rough alien told me to steer clear.

"Doesn't look like you're doing any salvage right now," I pointed out. "You can't possibly take the whole ship for yourself."

"My family will arrive soon, and the looting will begin." His voice held so much confidence that I knew he was lying. Nobody is that certain about anything. "We do not need your help."

Another look at the sensors. No sign of anyone coming to help him. Or me.

"You're sitting in the only ship your family owns," I said, wincing at the flare of anger in his eye. My mouth kept going while my brain listened, mortified. "My father made sure of that when he rammed the *Second Dusk*."

He leaned back in his seat, and I realized he wasn't wearing anything on his broad, muscular chest. The sight was very distracting—Krell's deep blue skin rose and fell with his breathing, and I imagined nestling against him, my head resting on his chest, listening to his heart beating.

I blinked, shivered, and tried to keep those unwanted thoughts out of my mind. At least Krell was too busy staring at me to notice how distracted I was. It took me a moment to realize why—I hadn't had a chance to replace my t-shirt yet. Blood rushed to my cheeks and I could have melted into my seat with embarrassment.

Did he have a similar accident to mine, or does he just go topless all the time? I tried to distract myself with humor to stop myself dying of shame, and I leaned closer to the camera so all it showed was my face as I pressed on.

"Neither of us is getting out of here alone. Best case, one of the big salvage corps arrives in time to 'rescue' us and claim our ships as salvage in exchange for dumping us at the nearest station." I'd make it home from there but losing the *Stardancer* would ruin my family. Watching Krell's face as he did the math for himself, I saw him come to the same conclusion.

Krell didn't like that any more than I did. "Then we have no choice but to bare our weaknesses to each other. I arrived in the swarm, and it left my ship crippled, the engine and sensors dead, life support barely functional. I barely made it here. How has yours fared? Can we escape this trap together?"

The damage to my life support worried me. For me and Freefall, it would do, but add a Hormza to the mix? It wouldn't last the months it would take to fly home in realspace. My breath stuck in my chest, and I licked my dry lips nervously. I had to force myself to reply. *Please, please let the answer be yes.* "Does your hyperdrive still work?"

A heartbeat of silence. I gripped the patched and

taped arms of my chair tight enough for my knuckles to go white.

"It does. But without engines, it is useless." I couldn't read him well, but I thought I saw the mirror to my hope in his one good eye.

"Mine is a wreck, but I've got engines," I said, watching him exhale. As the stress left him, I couldn't help noticing how handsome he really was. *Not now, Izzy!* "My life support should be enough for a couple of days. If you can reach me with your hyperdrive—"

"—and it's compatible with your systems," Krell said, baring his sharp, predator's teeth in what I hoped was a smile.

"We can both get home," we finished together.

The rush of that decision carried me most of the way through planning how we'd make it work. Krell swore he could bring the hyperdrive to me, much safer than me bringing the Stardancer closer and risking more damage. It still sounded insane for him to jump the distance between us and join me, but I had to trust him when he said he could do it.

Trust him. That was the problem. He was a sworn enemy of my family and I'd be all alone with him in the *Stardancer.* While the thought of spending a week alone with him sent a tingle through me, my rational brain balked. If Krell decided to throw me out of the airlock, into vacuum

I'd go. I'd put up a fight, sure, but I doubted I'd even slow him down.

He has to trust me too, I told myself. *If I don't open the airlock for him, he'll die out there and I can grab the hyperdrive off his corpse.*

The thought made me shudder, a visceral horror shaking me from my toes to the top of my head. Dying out there in the icy embrace of space was a nightmare. Krell would hang there, waiting for his suit's airscrubbers to run down, the air in his helmet thickening...

Serves him right. I heard my dad as though he was in the copilot's seat, his voice rough and ragged from one too many close calls with vacuum. Carl Dorran held his grudges as dear as his children and wouldn't miss a chance to do his enemies harm. *That alien motherfucker doesn't deserve your air supply, Isadora. And you don't have the spare capacity to waste.*

"Shut up, Dad," I said under my breath. "This isn't your decision."

An imagined dry chuckle was all the answer I got, but it was enough. The feud between our families had lasted three generations—I'd grown up with it and so had Krell. Like it or not, neither of us would make our decision alone. We all carried a part of our family with us.

The transfer itself was difficult for both of us. I had to hold the Stardancer in position above the *Third Sunrise* without getting hit by any debris large enough to do more damage, and I had the easy job. Fingers dancing across the controls, I gave the *Stardancer* little nudges, holding her steady relative to the broken hull of the battleship. The explosion in the *torpedo magazine* had stripped away the plating, leaving only a skeletal framework of jagged metal struts. Somehow, Krell had wedged his ship on the inside of that twisted mess. It must have seemed like a great choice, safe from the flying shrapnel that had crippled both of our vessels. Unfortunately, if I tried to fly the Stardancer in there, I'd be more likely to impale her on the exposed struts than dock with the *Third Sunrise.*

A tiny dot grew from *Third Sunrise*, pushed by small sprays of gas. Krell, ascending to meet me with the grace of a pouncing cat. Behind him, starlight gleamed off the mirror-bright surface of the hyperdrive he towed.

One stray piece of space junk and he'd end up smeared across the Elder battlefield.

"You'd better not have fucked this up," I said, though he couldn't hear me. "If I'm going to all this effort and your hyperdrive goes flying into the dark, I'm screwed."

The alien came closer, closer, and I tried not to stare at the screen tracking him. My job was keeping the ship steady and undamaged, giving Krell a stationary target to aim for. Attention darting from screen to screen, I shifted the bare minimum needed to dodge anything large enough to do more than scuff the paintwork. That took enough of my concentration that Krell almost reached me before I spotted what was wrong. He wasn't wearing a space suit.

A fine tracery of ice lined his blue skin, and his jaws were wide as though to snap shut on his prey. The thought of being that prey made me shiver with a weird mix of anticipation and fear. That he was still alive added awe to the mix. A human trying that? Dead in thirty seconds. Somehow Krell was still going, conscious enough to use a handheld thruster to steer and accelerate toward the *Stardancer*.

Normally—if you'd call any jump from ship to ship normal—I'd have maneuvered more freely, knowing that even if he missed, I could come around for another pass to pick him up. Not this time. Without a suit, even Krell wouldn't live long enough to match vectors with, and in this chaotic mess I wouldn't trust my sensors to keep track of him. We had one shot at this, no more. Better to risk another impact from a piece of flying junk than to risk Krell missing because I dodged too far out of the way.

So I gritted my teeth, focused on my work, and accepted the smaller hits while I dodged the big ones. It sounded like a rainstorm hitting the hull and

I had an uncomfortable image of the paint stripping away, then the hull, and finally me. I did my best to put that out of my mind, focusing on tracking objects large enough to wreck the ship and keep out of their way as much as possible.

A loud clang filled the ship, and my blood froze. Had I missed something?

No. A glance at the monitors showed me it was Krell hitting the hull. Heart in my throat, I watched as he bounced off. Grabbed desperately for the ship.

Caught hold.

And pulled himself into the waiting airlock, towing the cylindrical hyperdrive inside after him and shutting the outer hatch. As soon as he was inside, I opened the throttle, pushing the *Stardancer* into the safest course out of this nightmarish vortex of death. I didn't need to worry about my passenger —as soon as the sensors reported a lifesign in the airlock, automatic systems kicked in and flooding it with air. I glanced at the airlock camera, just in time to see Krell slumping to the deck. Apparently that jump had taken its toll after all, though his vital signs were stable. My enemy, my family's sworn foe, was now just one door away, and once he'd recovered, he'd open it and step through.

Why did that send warm tingles radiating through my body? It wasn't anger that filled me, it wasn't fear that made my limbs weak. No, it was anticipation that made my heart flutter. I was too busy piloting to think about the reasons for those feelings, and I embraced that excuse with a passion. Swooping past the engine parts I'd claimed earlier, I engaged the tractor beam and took it in tow as we passed. That would have to be enough to pay for repairs—no way I was stopping for anything more.

The Stardancer was nearly out of the debris field when the airlock sensors registered movement. Krell, pulling himself to his feet. After his ridiculous jump, I'd expected him to need hours of rest at the very least, but the Hormza warrior was even hardier than I'd thought.

Swallowing, I glanced at the airlock controls. One touch would turn that green light red and lock Krell in the airlock. Another would open the outer door an inch, venting the air into space and killing him. At which point I'd take the hyperdrive from his corpse, just like dad would have wanted.

"No." I said it firmly, ignoring my father's imagined disappointment. "I won't murder someone just because of his family, Dad. Besides, I went to the trouble of putting another t-shirt on, and I won't waste that effort by murdering the only person who'll see me."

I just hoped that Krell made the same choice. He had to, because if he didn't, I'd die.

This is insane. Who the hell lets a battle-hardened alien warrior board their ship willingly? I watched the airlock cycle. If I wanted to keep Krell outside, this was my last chance. Once the inner door opened, he'd have me cornered and helpless.

A chime announced the opening of the airlock, and the last chance to keep him out had slipped through my fingers. Dad had insisted I take a stunstick in case of trouble, but I had no illusions about my skill with it. If it came to a fight, I'd already lost.

"Better get this over with," I told myself, checking the radar again. Nothing near our course, not anymore. The autopilot would keep me safe just fine, leaving me free to greet my 'guest.' After a moment's thought, I left the stunstick holstered by the pilot's seat. Carrying it was more likely to antagonize Krell than deter him.

The airlock opened onto the crew deck, the largest room on the *Stardancer* aside from the hold. Space enough for six to eat together, a chipped and worn table for them to eat at. In better times, my family sat around it, laughing or bickering, but no longer. In the months since I'd last shared this space with anyone, I'd gotten used to having it to myself. The idea of sharing it with a stranger made me skittish.

Especially this alien, who awoke so many conflicting feelings in my heart. I looked up at him, framed in the airlock doorway, and my jaw dropped as I got my first good look at him. At his scarred face, one good eye raking the room, looking for threats. His broad shoulders, the muscular torso that made my heart race, abs I could have stared at for hours. And he'd not made even a token effort to hide them. He wore nothing above the waist, and why not? Anyone with a body that gorgeous should show it off if he wanted to.

Thankfully, he did wear clothes below the waist, though his pants left little to the imagination. Skin-tight black material molded to his powerful thigh muscles and did nothing to conceal the massive bulge between his legs. Blood rushed to my cheeks, and I bit my lip as I pulled my gaze back to his face. We looked at each other, wordless tension rising, and I struggled to find something to say. At last, I drew a deep breath to welcome him aboard with some clumsy cliche.

Just in time to hear an angry yowl from off to one side as Freefall launched herself at the alien warrior like an orange-furred missile. My heart dropped and everything seemed to slow down as she sailed toward Krell's face. I tried to shout something, anything, to stop Krell from doing the obvious and treating this as an attack.

I had no time. Krell's reflexes were too fast, and Freefall was on him before I'd drawn breath. Krell's hand came up to snatch the cat out of the air.

And then he fell backward with an exaggerated cry of pain, holding the fuzzball above his face and doing a spirited impression of a man attacked by forces too great to fight off. If he wanted me to take him seriously, though, he should have done a better job of suppressing his laughter.

"I surrender! Mighty hunter, you have me." Krell tried, and failed, to keep a straight face as he set Freefall down on his chest. He turned his gaze to me with a rakish grin. "Izzy, will you call off your creature?"

My turn to laugh. "Freefall is a cat, and which of us owns the other is an open question. But fine, I'll save you from her."

The tension well and truly gone, I felt safe enough to approach and retrieve the ginger cat. I'd have offered a hand to the fallen alien, but he didn't need my help. He bounced to his feet instantly, reaching out to scratch Freefall behind the ears and winning a purr.

"You have a fierce warrior to protect you."

"Fierce, yes. Effective? You seem to have bought her loyalty with skritches. Now what?" I asked. Close enough to smell his scent, the urge to find out what his skin felt like was almost irresistible. If my arms hadn't been full of cat, I don't think I'd have held back.

Fortunately, Krell's arms were empty. He made use of that, too, stroking my cheek with one hand and setting off fireworks inside me. A gasp escaped my lips, and I looked up into his eyes.

"I meant, uh," I trailed off before my objection really began. Did I want to talk him out of this?

Hell no. My inner voice was not shy about what I wanted, and the proper manners mother had tried to drum into me could protest all they liked. Here I stood next to eight feet of raw sexual attraction, and I didn't intend to say no to the chance.

Krell's mechanical eye whirred, focusing in on me, and he cocked his head to the side. After a moment of tense stillness, I realized he was waiting for me—a sign that I truly wanted this. *Gosh, a sexy space pirate who cares about consent? Where have you been all my life?*

I didn't keep him waiting. Putting Freefall down, I reached out and ran my fingers down Krell's chest. His skin felt different, inhuman, and somehow that was a surprise. A rougher texture than human skin, subtle differences to the muscles and bones beneath. I wanted to explore every inch of him and note the differences.

For science, of course.

His fingers slid across my cheek and into my hair, and his grin widened as he drew me toward him. Our lips touched, and the kiss sent lighting through me. No more thoughts, no more lies to myself. I wrapped my arms around his neck, my legs around his waist, and gave the kiss everything I had.

Krell's free hand grabbed my ass, squeezing and supporting me. I instantly regretted my decision to wear pants.

"Bunks that way," I gasped when our lips reluctantly parted. Krell followed my outstretched finger and nodded, carrying me to the door that slid open at our approach.

Lights flickered on, showing the bunkroom off in all its chaos. When we'd flown out as a family, it had been a tight squeeze, but it was too much space for me alone. As usual, junk expanded to fill the space available—clothes lay on the floor and the spare bunks, along with empty food containers and scattered hologram displays.

I should have tidied, a panic-stricken voice inside me insisted.

Be fair. I didn't exactly expect to have company over.

If the mess bothered Krell, he didn't show it. His kisses became more forceful, more urgent, as he carried me to my bunk and set me down. I sank into the soft mattress and groaned, trying to hold on to him when he pulled back.

Impossible. His strength was too much for me to restrain, and he gently disentangled himself to stand over me, looking like some kind of sexy war god.

"Undress," he told me. The casual power of his words had me obeying before I thought about it, and his arrogant smirk when he realized that somehow made him sexier. I ought to be annoyed. Hell, I *was* annoyed. But waves of desire rocked me, drowning out any resentment, and I didn't waste time arguing.

He wanted me naked. I wanted me naked. The

rest? Details. I pulled my t-shirt over my head and threw it aside, blushing as Krell watched intently. Unfastening my pants, I wriggled out of them, giving him a show. The low, hungry growl I got from him in response would have been enough evidence that he enjoyed it, even without the swelling in his pants. I swallowed, wondering if he could really be that big.

Time to find out. "Your turn," I told him.

He laughed, touching the fastening on his belt. The tight leather-like pants vanished like a dream on waking. One second there, clear as day, the next, no more than a memory. I blinked at the sight, but the magical technology didn't distract me from what it revealed. Nothing would have.

Eyes wide, I stared at his cock. I'd known it would be huge, but this? Incredible. Unbelievable. The long heavy weight of it pulsed as I watched, shape shifting according to some pattern that I couldn't understand. A spur stuck out above it and ridges grew and shrank along its length. My body trembled when I imagined that buried inside me, the spur perfectly placed to touch my clit as that pulsing shaft filled me. Though surely that monster of a cock wouldn't fit?

Maybe, maybe not, but goddamn, I'm going to find out.

Krell's long, low growl made me shiver with something that wasn't quite fear. Like I was the mouse who wanted to be caught by the cat.

I slipped off my panties, he cast away his boots and harness, and then we were both naked. His gaze slid up and down my body, and I shivered. It took an effort not to cover myself, to hide, but I resisted the urge. It wouldn't have been fair, not when I was drinking in the sight of that magnificent alien body.

The moment stretched out until, at last, Krell lowered himself to crouch beside my bed, leaning in to plant the lightest, sweetest kiss I could imagine on my lips. My heart racing, I reached up to pull him closer, sliding my fingers through his quills and trying to pull him closer to me.

Krell had other ideas, and the strength to ignore my hands as I tried to guide him. Instead, he lifted his lips from mine, ignoring my whimpered protest to move to my neck. Whimpers turned to moans as he planted kisses there, and when he bit me, I arched and gasped and moaned.

Krell chuckled, scraping predator-sharp teeth across my skin again. "You like that."

It wasn't a question. He spoke it with conviction, and he wasn't wrong. I tried to say something, anything, but all I could manage was a strangled moan.

Perhaps Krell took that as a protest or a challenge. He continued kissing my neck as his hands explored their way down my body, caressing my breasts, roaming down over my stomach. Moving so slowly, deliberately, delicately, that I wanted to scream at him.

But then he might *stop*.

And that wouldn't do at all.

Finally slipping his hand between my legs, running a tantalizing finger along my pussy lips before sliding between them. I arched and moaned again as he rubbed me oh-so-lightly, teasing and tormenting.

"You do like it," Krell whispered into my ear. "You're as wet as the ocean."

Heat spread across my face, down my neck, across my breasts. As true as his words were, I didn't want to admit it. Instead of an answer, ran my fingers down his abs, the strange texture of his skin delighting me. He growled again, and I recognized the longing in that sound. I'd been making it seconds carlicr.

"And you're as hard as diamond," I gasped when my fingers strayed down to touch his cock, exploring him. Krell shuddered as I brushed the small spur, and it vibrated against my fingers. My jaw dropped at the thought of that pressing against my clit as he rode me.

"Never said I didn't like it," he said, rough undertones in his voice. Pulses ran up and down the length of his shaft and I stroked him. trying to match the rhythm. Krell growled.

"If you keep doing that, I will lose control."

"Do you think I want you in control?"

"I might damage you."

"You won't." This time I was the one to speak with unearned confidence—something made me sure I was safe with this man, despite his monstrous strength, razor claws, and pointed teeth. Safer than I'd ever felt with a human.

Krell pulled back, my hand slipping from his cock as he withdrew. Before I had a chance to object, he'd bent over me again, kissing and nipping at my breasts while his left hand kept rubbing my pussy, teasing my clit, making me arch and squirm. Planting kisses down my body, he at last came to my pussy, replacing his fingers with his tongue.

I screamed at his touch, the pleasure overwhelming me. There was something magical about his rough, eager tongue, an incredible sensation no human could match. The texture, perhaps? I didn't know, I didn't care, I just didn't want him to stop. Grabbing at his head, I took hold of his horns and pulled him against me. Each touch of his tongue made me thrash wildly, and he was my only anchor.

This time, he let me guide him, steering his head by the horns. I knew he could have ignored me, that his strength would be too much for me if he wanted to take control.

He didn't. He wanted me to feel safe, to know that he wouldn't do anything I didn't want. And I sure didn't mind that, as long as he kept doing the things I *did* want.

It didn't take long for that magnificent, wonderful, magical tongue of his to push me to the edge of orgasm. At the last moment, I looked down at Krell, only to see him looking back at me. My gaze met his and the intensity of that pushed me into the onrushing orgasm. I cried out again, pulling on his horns and shuddering as wave after wave of pleasure rocked my body.

I didn't know how long I was in the throes of passion, but when I recovered enough to focus again, Krell loomed over me, watching me with a smile. A *smug* smile, but I didn't mind that. He'd earned the right to be pleased with himself.

"You taste amazing, Izzy," he said, kissing his way up my body. "And you make such wonderful noises."

Blood rushed to my cheeks at that, but I didn't argue. Instead, I pulled him to me, onto the bed. The bunk under us creaked ominously with his added weight, but I didn't care. I wanted him, I needed him, and nothing else mattered.

From the way he came at me, I knew Krell felt the same way. Kissing his way up my body, giving me gentle bites as he went, he slid between my legs, monster cock pressing against me. And stopped, meeting my eyes again.

Heart pounding, scared and exhilarated in equal

measure, I gave him the tiniest of nods. Almost before I'd finished, he thrust. Thrust *hard,* his cock stretching me as he drove home, making me arch under him and gasp with a pleasure that was almost pain.

Almost, but not quite. Instead, it was the most intense joy I'd ever experienced. I'd thought Krell's tongue was good, and it *was,* but it didn't compare to his dick.

Wrapping my legs around his waist, I urged him deeper, biting my lip as he grew even bigger inside me, pulsing slowly. Back arching, I gripped him tight and he roared, an animal sound that burned straight through my conscious mind and into the buried ancestral memories. Krell was a predator, and I was his prey, and *damn,* I liked that.

The spur above his cock pressed against my clit as he drove deep, and its vibration was almost too much. I dug my nails into Krell's back, panting and shaking, and Krell roared again, thrusting deeper and harder, until we both teetered on the edge of a mind-shattering climax.

A final thrust made me scream and thrash as the world dissolved around us. Krell came too, our bodies locked together in that incredible moment of pleasure. My universe shrunk to nothing but *him,* his marvelous, monstrous cock buried inside me, his vibrating spur pressed to my clit and driving me into orgasm after incredible orgasm.

It seemed to take hours. It felt like seconds. I had no idea how much time passed before my thoughts took coherent form again. Krell still filled me, held me to him, his sweat-slick blue skin glistening. His breathing came hard and fast and his pulse raced as he recovered. I wasn't doing any better, my heart pounding. My head flopped back, and I focused on breathing until the room came back into focus.

Something was wrong, though I couldn't put my finger on it at first. Everything sat at an odd angle, and it nagged at my consciousness until I gave in and looked around. Scattered, torn bedclothes added to the mess now, and it took me a moment to notice what had happened.

Somewhere in that last, passionate embrace, Krell's weight and the power of his thrusts had torn my bunk loose from the wall. And I hadn't even noticed.

"Good thing there are spare bunks," I muttered under my breath. I didn't mean for Krell to hear, but he chuckled and held me tight.

"Yes," he agreed. "We can do this five times more before we run out."

Krell and I lay in the ruins of my bunk, still wrapped around each other, our hearts racing as though we'd run a marathon. My throat hurt, raw from the screams of joy my alien lover had forced from me. I ached where his fingers had gripped tight enough to bruise. My muscles burned from exertion.

I'd never felt happier. If those minor pains were the price of sharing my bed with Krell, I'd pay it gladly. Though we'd run out of bunks to share in a hurry.

My laughter at that thought got Krell to open his eyes and raise a quizzical eyebrow. "What is so funny, Izzy?"

My heartbeat had *just* calmed down. His growling tone started it racing again, and my cheeks heated. "Nothing, really. I was just thinking about what I'm going to tell my family about this damage."

I gestured helplessly at the broken bunk, the shredded bedclothes, the chaos we'd caused in our coupling. Krell looked around too, his face darkening. Was that a blush, or did it mean something different in his species? There was so much about him I didn't know.

"You don't need to tell them," he said, speaking slowly as though feeling his way across a frozen lake and unsure if the ice would hold his words.

"Sure, I guess I can repair the bunk before I get home, but I don't have the tools to do it well. They'll notice, and even if they don't, there's nothing I can do about the sheets you tore. I'm just going to have to face the music."

"No." Krell spoke with such finality that I

couldn't help shutting up. "I did not mean you should conceal it from your kin. I meant..."

He trailed off there, the self-assurance with which he'd started speaking already gone by the time he finished. Muscles tensed under his skin, and I bit my lip, waiting for him to finish.

"I meant I will tell them." Now his words came out fast, bitten off. As though he was afraid of my reaction, but that was ridiculous. This was a man who'd jumped from one ship to another *without a spacesuit.*

The silence between us stretched out, awkwardness filling the room. Krell's forehead wrinkled, his lips tightening as he watched me. This mattered to him, and I swallowed, trying to find the right answer.

All that came to me was a question. "What do you want to say to my family?"

I winced at the sound of my voice. I'd tried for a calm and reassuring tone and hit nervous and breathless instead.

"That you are my mate, and if they object..." He paused there, visibly rephrasing his statement before continuing. "If they object, *I will listen respectfully,* but the decision is yours and mine, not theirs."

I swallowed again, my cheeks burning and breath catching. It took no effort at all to understand what he'd intended to say—Krell would have no issue with fighting my family. Still, I was glad he'd stopped himself. As trouble filled as my relationship with my parents was, I wasn't at the point of wishing harm on them.

But the thought brought the reality of our situation home to me. A shadow fell over the warmth that filled me.

"Are you planning to stay with us, then?"

Krell's frown deepened. "No, little one, I must return to my kinfast. I shall take you with me and together we shall make a fine home for our family."

"That won't work," I said, pulling back from him and trying to close off my emotions. "I have family too, and I won't just abandon them."

"Honorless slugs that don't deserve you. Come with me and we'll build a better family together."

Folding my arms, I gave Krell a look that ought to have burned a hole through him and the bulkhead behind him. "All the bad things your kin tell you about the Dorans, I've heard about the Kyrossi. Your cousin broke my sister's leg!"

"After she sabotaged a trade deal he'd spent half a standard year setting up. She got off lightly."

We glared at each other, faces flush with anger rather than desire. Long, heavy seconds passed before Krell raised his hands. "Peace! Whatever stories we trade about each other's kin, you are proof not all Dorani are monsters. I'll take your word that your kin are better than I've been taught."

"And you're proof that your clan aren't all rampaging pirates," I admitted in a slightly wistful tone. Part of me wouldn't have minded being taken as a pirate's prize. "So maybe it's time this stupid feud ended?"

Every time I thought Krell's frown was at its deepest, he proved me wrong. "What do you mean? My kin will never surrender to yours."

"Nor mine to yours," I agreed. "But, well, how are they going to compete with us? You have no ship, and without one, how long can you hold out against the big guilds?"

"About as long as your kin will manage without a hyperdrive."

"Exactly. If our families carry on the feud, we're all ruined. The only way out of it is together."

Krell froze at that, and I swore I could hear the crunch of gears shifting in his head. Was that my euphoria talking? Or did I really have something?

When Krell's frown lifted, it was like watching the sun creep over a planet's horizon from orbit. His brow cleared, his hands flexed as though he was grappling with the problem, and his lips parted into a grin that made his eye sparkle.

"Everyone will hate that. Your kin, my kin, *everyone.*"

"Yes. Scared of a fight?"

That surprised him into a booming laugh that shook the room. "Isadora Maria Doran, you are going to get me into so much trouble."

"Oh, I *do* hope so," I said, laughing with him. We

had a plan, then. And I knew exactly how I wanted to celebrate.

Launching myself at him, I almost caught my fearsome warrior by surprise. Almost. His reflexes kicked in at the last second, and he spun me around, kissing me and squeezing me gently. I squirmed against him, kissing back passionately, arms and legs wrapped around his torso and leaving no doubt what I wanted.

"Again? Are Earthwomen insatiable?" Krell laughed with a rough and lusty undertone.

"Don't know," I answered, and sank my teeth into his neck, muffling my next words. "No one's managed it yet."

"A warrior does not shy from such a challenge," Krell informed me with all the dignity he could manage while being gnawed on by an eager, wriggling Earthwoman. "Which of these bunks is most expendable?"

My heart fluttered, and I moaned as I gestured. *Oh, this is going to be a fun journey home.*

MORE FROM LESLIE

We hope you enjoyed ***Star Crossed*** by Leslie Chase!

Read more of Leslie's spicy alien romance in *Auric,* Book One of the *Crashland Colony* Romances.

Crashed on an unexplored planet, with only an alien warrior and a holographic cat for company… what's a girl to do?

Tamara expected the trip to Arcadia Colony to be safe and boring. And it is — until an impossibly hot alien warrior crashes into the ship, bringing a warning that only Tamara believes. Helping the rugged alien means mutiny... but the threat he's warning about is worse.

Auric turned his back on the Silver Band when they abandoned honor in favor of piracy. Drawn by the riches of the colony ship, the Band are on their way — and once they arrive, the humans are doomed. Now that he's met Tamara, Auric knows he can't let anything happen to her. She's the woman fate has chosen for him, the woman he would give his life to save.

When the humans and their alien attackers are stranded on a forbidden planet, Auric and Tamara are flung together on a journey to find other survivors. Will fate be enough to keep Auric and Tamara together? Or will the dangers of the planet tear them apart?

Born in London, living in Scotland, and dreaming of space, Leslie writes delicious and dangerous aliens and the Earthwomen who love them.

WWW.LESLIE-CHASE.COM

OF TENTACLES AND FIN

BY V.T. BONDS

OF TENTACLES AND FIN

V.T. BONDS

SARAH

THIS IS THE END. Whatever dreams I may have aspired to live, whatever hopes I had for the future, they were all for naught.

I will not live past sunrise.

The gentle sway of the ocean under my life raft neither inspires comfort nor dread in me. It just is. It's another part of my demise—another piece of the backdrop for my anticlimactic death.

If the dastardly and temperamental ocean had stuck to the plan, then I'd be on a happy little island, watching the waves lap at a sandy beach while sipping a margarita under a colorful umbrella. Instead, I'm trapped on a bright yellow emergency raft with no food, water, or protection from the sun. I have no idea where I've drifted to, or what happened to the other eight people who'd been on the little charter boat with me.

I did my best to prevent sunburn yesterday by wrapping my dress over me like a tarp, but even in the dark I see bright red strips on my feet where they escaped the meager protection. The printed flowers already look faded from the bleaching power of the sun, and I swear my ass will forever boast the pattern from the bottom of the boat, since I don't even have underwear to protect me.

Not that forever will be very long, since my time of living slowly comes to an end.

Untying the thin material from my waist, I prepare to drape it over my head again, for however many hours I have left before dehydration kills me.

I don't want to die, but after crying for hours, my body refuses to produce more tears, so I settle into reality and accept the inevitable.

Where were dastardly pirates at a time like this, ready to swoop in and rescue a damsel in distress so they could ravish her?

Drifting in and out of awareness, I let my dreams bring me my fantasies, each one warped and taboo, yet soothing in the end as I find happiness, love, and devotion.

Years have proven my favorite romance reads are as fiction as my imagination, for even though I yearn for love, my every attempt has ended in failure.

And I've tried. A lot.

A splash startles me, the eerie sensation of being watched forcing my heart into my throat. I rise to my knees, grabbing the lip of the raft and searching the horizon for rescue.

Except, why am I looking far away, when the sound was most definitely nearby?

Movement streaks across my periphery, and I dart my focus toward it, the hammering of my heart drowning out the gentle sounds of water shifting against my lifeboat. Something large sinks below the surface of the ocean, and my fear skyrockets my heartrate into the stratosphere.

I'd rather die a slow and boring death than be eaten by a shark or swallowed by a whale.

The raft bucks under me, forcing me to grab the side with both hands or fly into the water, and I lean backward, hoping with every fiber of my being the raft rights itself. If it tips, I'm a goner.

My scream bounces off the water and disappears in the wind. As the boat rocks toward normalcy, my eyes deceive me.

Pitch black orbs rise from the depths of the ocean, surrounded by shimmery purple flesh, gills, and teeth. Too humanoid for my liking, yet too monstrous to be real, the creature closes the distance between us so quickly my scream still pierces the air as it breaks the surface. Silk wraps around my throat as the abomination reaches up and reveals his long, powerful extremities.

Other tentacles wind around my forearms and shoulders, pushing me until my back hits the rough surface of the raft. My lungs fill with oxygen and I scream again, reality fading away as I stare up into insanely intelligent eyes, the knowledge I sense lurking within my attacker more frightening than the thought of being ripped apart by a shark.

A fragrance burrows into my nostrils, something rich and masculine and full of power, and my scream dies as heat fills my belly.

Insanity settles over me as I freeze, instincts warning me to go statue still in hopes of appeasing the predator pinning me down.

Salty liquid drips from the beast holding me hostage, his myriad of tentacles sliding around my legs and pushing my untied dress off my stomach. Surprisingly soft fingers brush against my cheekbone after his countless tentacles part to reveal two human arms.

The deepest vibration I've ever heard leaves his chest and seeps into my marrow, melting my bones and heating my core. His mouth moves, but the language he speaks makes no sense, and I lay frozen in terror and confusion as he brushes his smooth cheek against my own.

He moves so fast I don't even have time to flinch, his sharp teeth piercing the juncture of my left shoulder and neck. Poison sears into my bloodstream, sending agony streaking throughout my entire body, and I writhe under the assault. My brain splits in two as it revolts, one half refusing to believe this is happening while the other fights with all it has.

I push and kick, but the creature doesn't budge, his hold on me barely allowing me to wriggle against the thrashing raft. He lifts his teeth from my neck and smooths his scorching tongue up my wound, the coppery scent of my blood mingling with his masculine pheromones.

"Mine."

A startled sob rips from my chest as his word registers, but pain steals my ability to respond. My lungs seize as tiny monsters eat at my throat and chest, and somewhere deep in my addled brain I recognize the signs of change. The air becomes too dry, too coarse, and the wind buffets my ears in the most unpleasant way.

"Oursss."

My back bows as he hisses the word into my ear and runs a tentacle over my wound. Locked in his innumerable grasps and fighting for breath, I have no choice but to writhe in agony as he rolls sideways, leading the way into the ocean.

As my mind screams in terror, we fall into another world, and I fight harder, not wanting to drown. He holds me tighter, sliding more tendrils of control around me.

My dress billows around us, the currents tugging it this way and that, until deft digits slide it off my body, the mixture of human hands and flexible tentacles too much to process. Tiny, round spots pepper my body, shielding me from the cool water as the suction cups on his tendrils search my flesh.

After watching my dress whip away into the blue, I latch my gaze on the surface and struggle to swim upward, knowing my captor won't let me go but desperate to breathe air. My lungs burn from lack of oxygen and my head throbs as though it may burst, but I hold my breath, dreading the alternative.

Black orbs block my view of the fading sun, the streaks of light dancing in the waves turning to murky gray as we descend further away from escape. With a maniacal glee pulling at his lips, the monster wraps an extra tentacle around my naked chest and squeezes, forcing the air from my lungs. The first bubble leaves me, tickling my cheek as it floats up my face, and with my last chance of survival stolen from me, I scream.

Angry and terrified and desperate, I push my every emotion into the sound and put off inhaling the salty ocean for as long as I can.

Shiny white teeth flash as he loosens his hold on my chest and rubs a limb over a tender spot under my collarbone. He flicks a flap of skin that wasn't there a few moments ago, and I jolt as cold water seeps into my chest. At the same time, he lowers his lips to mine and claims my mouth, prying my teeth open with tongue and tentacles, and invading one of my most intimate places with ruthless intent. Salty water rushes down my throat, but although it isn't comfortable, I don't suffer the agony I expect.

My muscles seize as icy heat pulses from my lungs outward, infecting every organ within my body until not a single cell remains the same. Even as my heart keeps pumping and my diaphragm forces water in and out of my lungs, I feel swamped and wrong, my brain refusing to come to terms with my ability to breathe water.

I can't have gills. Five seconds ago I was prepared to die a slow death. This must just be a dying woman's last hallucination.

Yet warm ropes wrap around me, plucking at my nipples and testing the flesh around my upper thighs.

"Hush, hush, my pretty pale one. This is only the beginning, but I'll take care of you. I know better now, I promise."

Now that we're underwater, his voice seems smoother and impossibly deeper, almost as though he aims straight for the weak spot I never knew I had hidden behind my sternum.

I don't want his help. I don't want his touch. I want to go back up to my little raft and pretend like this isn't happening.

He lowers his mouth back to mine and pries me open again, his tentacles too strong for me to deny them, and as he plunders the recesses, he sets up a rhythm as old as time. I push at his shoulders to no avail, hating how my nipples tighten and my womb clamps down as he teases the crease between my thigh and my folds.

More change sweeps through me, awakening parts of my body I've never acknowledged, and I cry as my insides beg for relief. My stomach cramps and throbs, sending streaks of desire between my breasts and my core, and my clit swells and grows so sensitive my own folds feel too rough. Jerking and flailing, I try to get away from him, but physics work differently in this new world and I lose against his superior strength.

Human fingers invade my intimate folds, sliding along the outsides of my petals before seeking the extremely sensitive bundle of nerves at the top of my mound. With a scorching thumb mashing my clit against my body, he thrusts two fingers into my opening. Electricity spears into my abdomen, the ruthless manhandling too much to ignore.

I fight off the pressure his stroking builds, but it grows as he sneaks the tip of a tentacle in alongside his fingers, my thrashing only aiding his violation. As he stretches my opening, he rumbles a groan into my mouth and scrambles what little sense I have left.

He pushes in and doesn't stop until agony flares deep within my abdomen.

Glass shards splinter through my reality as I break into a million pieces. I fly apart, shattering into the current to drift for eternity, the release too intense to call an orgasm.

Only his diabolical purr pulls me back together.

"Perfect, pale omega. You're ready. Swim."

His warmth disappears, leaving me stranded in frigid murkiness, and I float in a sea of confusion.

A humongous figure blocks out the faint sun from above, shocking me into panic. I glance upward but see nothing. Nothing for miles and miles. Looking down fills me with dread—pitch blackness hides whatever lurks beneath me.

Up. I must swim up.

The second I angle my body upright and bring my hands over my head to thrust myself upward, something brushes past my hip. I scream, my voice not at all how I expect—different but understandable—and twirl in hopes of seeing what torments me.

Nothing.

I kick and raise my arms again, wishing I were a more prolific swimmer, and set my sights on the surface.

It's too far away. I know I'll never make it, but I must try. I have no other option.

Something cold and rough slips along my torso before a force greater than anything I've ever felt knocks me sideways, stealing my upward momentum and spinning me in a disorienting twirl. Unable to tell which way is up, blinded by my hair and hurting from the hit, I panic. I thrash and flail, terrified of meeting whatever creature swept me aside with such force.

Rows of razor-sharp teeth flash by my face, followed by a barreled body so thick it blocks my entire vision for long, horrifying moments, stealing my ability to react. Frozen as though caught in an electrical current, I spin within the tiny whirlpool created by my new tormentor, my heart pounding in my head.

Intelligent, beady black eyes turn toward me, the open mouth gaping in a frightening smile as the shark creature aims his pointed nose at me.

Insanity returns full force, an irate voice in my head screaming in fury at the injustice. Myths tell mermen as charming and suave, not scarred, lethal, and malicious. The other, less hinged part of me scolds the first, correcting the assumption.

This is no merman. This is an abomination. Half shark, half... human soul? Besides the spark of intelligence in the pitch-black eyes, no human features lurk within the monster charging me.

Yet his smile grows as he flicks his tail and picks up speed, closing the distance between us. I scream and bat at the water around me, desperate to evade the glinting white razors heading my way. At the last second, he shifts his trajectory, knocking the brunt of his massive body against my flailing one, collapsing my chest as my skull cracks against hard muscle.

My vision turns fuzzy, but my nostrils fill with

decadence, the sharp, masculine pheromones cutting into my brain and arrowing to my womb before spreading to my extremities.

Before I regain my senses, I suffer another blow, except this time the creature stays pressed against me, and I'm swamped with fiery lust. The body propelling me forward offers so much bulk he expands wider than my shoulders, and his raw power feels more like a natural disaster than a singular being. His musk ruins my ability to recover as my blood boils, the ache I once knew as arousal nothing compared to the agony coursing through me. My skin sensitizes as lava heats my veins, the insistent throbbing of my core worse than the wounds on my neck.

His warmth disappears, leaving me ruined in his wake, stuck in confusion and terror.

Purple flesh, gills, and mocking eyes fill my vision before a guttural word spurs me into action.

"Swim."

Sobbing, unable to reconcile the cruel treatment I've suffered, I kick and struggle to gain my bearings, but agony spears into me.

Knives form a half circle over my right shoulder, the circumference so large it trails down from my neck to follow my spine before swooping below my shoulder blade and piercing along my shoulder. I scream as a matching row of knives sink into the corresponding flesh of my front, creating a half circle across my collarbone, down to hit soft tissue at the top of my chest before digging into the front of my shoulder. Meeting one gigantic, beady black orb with my right eye, a piece of my soul dies as my reflection's expression sinks deep into my psyche.

There's no escaping this reality.

Tentacles wrap around my forearms and press them to my torso as more grab my ankles and force them apart.

The water around me heats and shifts with such turbulence my skin shrivels, and a scorching body presses against my back. So unlike the barrel shape of seconds ago, the tapered waist of a human male and ridged abdominals slide against my bare flesh and reignite the fire in my veins.

Thick, coarse digits join the fray, sinking into my hips and holding me exactly where the beast behind me wants me.

I struggle against the limbs holding me, screeching in agony and misery as the shark monster drags two thick, rigid cocks across the globes of my ass. His snarl vibrates the teeth he's sunken into my shoulder, and my scream dies as my diaphragm refuses to relax.

Tentacles frame my face, holding my gaze hostage between two masculine, lust-crazed glares.

"Mine."

Nothing but the sounds of rushing water and rumbling chests reach my ears, but the word vibrates through my skull, the voice as deep as the first, but much smoother, like the surface of a frozen lake as my new captor speaks directly into my thoughts.

Agony blasts from my folds as an enormous cock spears its way into my entrance. Hips much bigger and stronger than mine force the invasion deeper into my womanhood as the beast behind me uses his bite on my shoulder and grip on my hips as leverage. Horrible relief mingles with terrified pain as he pushes so deep my core cramps in discomfort, but brutal pressure on my clit steals my scream. Something long, thick, and unyielding curves up from my entrance and hooks over the top of my pubic bone, and my hammering heart threatens to burst as I realize it's the second cock he brushed across my ass. It mashes my sensitive bundle of nerves so hard I feel his ruthless invasion twice, both in my abused channel and crushed clit.

Merciless fingers pluck at my nipples as unyielding tentacles hold me open for his intimate assault. The muscles pressed against my back flex, making his teeth tear the flesh of my shoulder, but an ominous growl ripples from the chest at my front and a rush of heat infects my bones.

I can't breathe. Can't move. Can't escape.

Again and again the monster behind me thrusts his hips, digging his cock deeper and deeper, until grunts accompany his movements. White teeth flash as my deep violet tormentor smirks, making me realize the sound comes from not only the creature behind me, but also from my own throat.

Tension grows within my abdomen, the unwanted lust coursing through my veins morphing agony into pleasure. The world around me fades, his brutal thrusts stealing every ounce of my focus. Despite my need to escape, anticipation fills me as he works toward easing the hunger in my womb.

Like gravel tumbling over itself, his purr pierces my eardrums and vibrates into my shoulder, taking over my chest and reaching deep into the muscle pumping blood throughout my veins. Something filthy blooms within my heart, and the violation of my soul tears a cry from my lips.

His cock grows impossibly bigger, stretching so large my channel sends streaks of agony up my spine and into my brain, and as he grunts next to my ear, he seats himself as deep into me as he can. My scream hurts my vocal cords, but I don't feel it. It's nothing compared to the agony in my womanhood as a distinct balloon wedges itself behind my pubic bone, inflating so large it seems to meet the cock clutched around the outside of my body.

Trapped between his savage instruments, I shatter as his release fills my womb, my organs cramping and muscles locking as rainbows of color flash across my vision.

Seconds turn into eternities. Agony becomes bliss. Darkness morphs into serenity.

I float in a field of cotton with the sun warming my skin.

Two voices intrude, both masculine and crude, yet their words become music lilting up to the big, puffy clouds meandering across the sky. Tentative fingers weave into mine as two warm, comforting bodies wrap themselves around my sides, joining me in the soft bed of grass.

Mine.

This is the dream I've dreamt my entire life—basking in the sun on a peaceful stretch of land, surrounded by love and support—except there was only ever one body pressed against mine. Never before have I had two companions. Two lovers. Two soulmates.

Cold trickles into my spine, slow and immeasurable, as reality intrudes. Gentle hands stroke my neck and continue down my sides in reassuring sweeps as my men murmur their praise.

Tears trail down my face. They spread.

A sluggish thud within my chest reverberates up my spine and into my brain.

My tears encompass my face, but don't stop there. They keep spreading.

A foreign word drifts into my ears, followed by the shriveling of my happiness.

My tears surround me, encasing my entire body in salty liquid, and with a shock, the truth runs through me.

I'm dying. These will be my last moments.

Worse than that, I'm dying between two monsters who've defiled my body.

Pain slices into my euphoria as teeth leave my flesh, but milliseconds later something warm and silky strokes along the wound, and the agony dissipates as though it never was. My eyes focus on the cloud of crimson hovering near my head, but I don't process it as my blood until eager lips suck it away.

"Our pale omega tastes divine."

With eyes so wide they ache, I meet glittery black orbs and stare at the octopus-like creature with slow, incomplete thoughts.

Not human. Evil. Pain. Wrong.

One word rises from within me so fast and sharp, my body jerks.

Mine.

Yet the blood in my veins grows stagnant and my peripheral vision fades.

"Swim, Zuk. She suffocates."

The creature behind me snarls and jerks his hips, torturing me since his weapon still remains locked within my body, but the edges of my vision dim further.

A resounding growl leaves the one in front of me, but he blips out of sight so fast my failing brain decides he was never there to begin with. My flesh pebbles as cool water rushes over it, and I decide I miss the warmth my captor encased me in.

The body pressed against my back stiffens, then undulates side to side, something almost sharp sweeping back and forth across my heels, and I realize its his fin as he swims.

My eyelids drift down, the single beat of my heart almost too much effort, but tendrils of warmth wrap around my head and pry my jaw open. As water rushes in, my lungs jolt into action, awakening every cell within my body.

I suck down lungful after lungful of water, the sensation of not needing to exhale odd and the outward flow from the flaps of flesh near my collar bone too weird to process. With reanimation, every complaint within my body makes itself known, my womb throbbing around the massive intrusion.

"Yes, see, I take good care of you. Good little omega. Swim."

Startled at the closeness of the voice, I open my eyes to find my tentacled tormentor leaning in to rub his face against mine. He slides his hold on my head around until there's a clear spot for his cheek to meet mine. His whisper sends curls of heat down my spine.

"Ours. Forever."

A groan sounds from behind me as the cock inside me jerks and troubles my insides with more of his release. With an influx of pressure on my clit, every nerve sparks to life, the hunger once sated now unfurling. Discomfort spears through the need as too much liquid fills my womb.

"Zuk, unmount her. My turn."

No. Mine.

"We do not want to damage our new omega like the last one. Finish."

No, Oktan. Too good. So soft.

Tentacles wrap around my upper thighs, their suction cups latching on and creating stinging rings on my vulnerable flesh. Oktan shifts to my side, wrapping another tentacle around my shoulders before sliding his human arms between me and Zuk.

"Yes. Now."

Despair grows behind my sternum as terrible pressure builds against my pubic bone, both from inside and outside of my body. An odd sound plays behind me, but my scream drowns it out as the pressure morphs to agony. The cock inside me deflates enough to slide into a most uncomfortable position, but it grinds along my channel until it rips from my opening.

Blinding pain streaks throughout my body, but when I instinctively try to curl into a ball, unrelenting tentacles hold me hostage yet again. A massive form darts over my head, and even with the pain distorting my vision, I blink in shock as I glimpse Zuk for the first time since he bit me.

With a terrifying mouthful of teeth, his grin reaches from one side of his face to the other, his neck as thick as his shoulders since it carries his dorsal fin, but below his arms resides a human torso. Bulkier than any creature has a right to be, his chiseled chest offers two ripped arms before narrowing into a perfect six pack. Between his hips sways the two massive cocks he ruined me with, but with rounded, distinct heads, veins running down the shafts, and each with definitive swollen sections near their base. Halfway down his thighs, his legs morph into a powerful fin, which he uses to whip around and speed back toward me.

Fear spikes my heartrate.

His grin widens.

Pain startles a shriek from me as something broad and rounded presses through my abused opening. Oktan's baritone groan vibrates into my back as he crams himself deep within my body, his invasion aided by another's violation.

Zuk rolls and slides his cheek along mine before allowing his momentum to carry him further down my body. With tentacles and fingers exploring every inch of my flesh and a gigantic, overly bumpy cock hammering my insides, Zuk grabs my shoulders and aligns his bellybutton with my face.

Two rigid dicks vie for my attention, and even though my palms reach out to push him away, a blast of vitality sweeps into my nostrils and annihilates whatever conscious thoughts I possess. Instead of accepting his guidance to savor his offerings with my tongue, I dart my mouth past his massive cocks.

Leading with my teeth, I give in to the urge caused by the invisible, gaping wound in my soul.

Mine.

I bite the flesh over his hip bone and grind my jaw, listening to his roar with sick satisfaction as a thorny vine springs to life between our hearts.

It *hurts*. More intimate than the vile acts they've forced me to endure, the connection between us leaves no part of our beings hidden.

I see into the dark recesses of his psyche while he pilfers my soul.

The flavor of his blood coats my tongue, both disgusting and decadent, and basal needs send it to my stomach as I swallow with relish.

Water swirls around us, making my hair an annoying, claustrophobic cloud around my head until deft ropes of muscle gather and clear it away from my face. Pressure on my scalp warns me of Oktan's attempt to pull me away, so I growl through the tough flesh between my teeth, not wanting to let it go.

Zuk's snarl accompanies sharp pinpricks as his nails bite into my scalp, his fingers weaving through the hold Oktan has on my hair before he yanks my face away. My bite loosens enough for his skin to remain attached to his body, but two uneven crescent wounds leak crimson into the salty ocean. I flick my tongue out and lap at my mark until he shifts his hips and crams the tip of his cock into my mouth.

I clench my jaw, intending to bite him where it will hurt the most, but fireworks explode across my tastebuds and animalistic sounds leak from my chest as my lips and tongue go to work. Licking and sucking, I demand all he can give me, lost in lust so thick cognizant thoughts can't move within the sludge.

A savage thrust from the beast behind me sends sharp streaks of agony into my abdomen, and I jerk within his hold, my body instinctively trying to escape despite how futile it may be. The hand on my scalp fists my hair while it's partner grabs my breast, Zuk's touch so different from Oktan's I don't need to see their hands on me to know which one torments me.

Something sharp brushes across my throbbing clit, and a shocked noise leaks around the cock in my mouth. In time with the deep, brutal hammering from my octopus monster, Zuk takes control of my skull, jabbing his cockhead into the back of my throat. When my abdominals tighten in response, Oktan's frantic pounding shatters me. He hits a place deep within my channel and causes a tidal wave. I buck and shriek as my release consumes me.

Zuk silences me with his member, shoving himself into my throat and growling as he fills my belly with his seed.

Oktan's cock morphs, his base thickening while

his shaft lengthens, and I hover on the edge of unconsciousness as the top half turns into innumerable branches. Several reach deeper until they encounter my cervix, and as his growl of completion rings in my ears, they pry the barrier open.

Every nerve in my body explodes as he stretches the entrance to my womb, his fattest extension popping into the unnatural opening and twitching as it pumps his seed directly into my uterus.

Blackness falls over my eyes, everything except the invasions of my body fading away as I search for the lovely meadow and bright sunshine I visited not long ago.

It never comes.

Shark teeth ghost across my clit as Zuk yanks his cock out of my throat. My reflexes suck down water, the sustenance clearing away the blackness across my vision.

"Our. Perfect. Pale. Omega," Oktan rumbles into my ear, each word emphasized with him mashing his groin against mine, causing his inhuman cock to swell and spurt more of his release into my womb.

Demanding limbs wrench my neck to an awkward angle even though I'm still locked in horrible pleasure, and after glimpsing Oktan's blissed out expression, purple flesh fills my vision.

Sandwiched between two brutes, my olfactory system singles out the one I have yet to claim. His rich, masculine scent strengthens my orgasm, and I fill my mouth with his flesh. Zuk scrapes his teeth across my clit again, forcing me into another seizure.

Unpleasant and yet satisfying, thick inky liquid coats my tongue and joins Zuk's seed in my belly.

Another vine springs to life, wrapping its thorns into my soul with such brutal force I sob.

I hate it. I need it. It hurts, but I'd suffer so much worse if it were to break.

Zuk's mountainous bulk leaves my front, abandoning my abused clit to diabolical tentacles. Oktan draws out my second orgasm by covering my clit with one of the suction cups on his rope of muscle. He manipulates it, and I die a theoretical death as he forces me into a third release. His ministration feels like sucking, pinching, biting, and a shock of electricity all rolled up into one.

Dazed, I don't resist when he extracts his depleted cock from my hole and guides my teeth out of his flesh.

The urge to crawl into bed and hide within a mound of blankets rises, so fierce a sob wrenches from my chest.

"Hush, our mate. You will have a nest. I have taken care of you—you still live, with both our marks."

Loosening his hold, Oktan maneuvers us until my vision fills with his muscular chest. Foreign desires demand I lean into him, but I refuse.

If shock had a time to show, now would be it, but

my senses stay sharp as my body trembles in pain and my mind slowly assembles the horrors I survived.

Murky sunlight dims as Zuk swims above us, his torso still human. His smug smile flashes across my view and I sob again, except anger rises quick and fierce. I long to lash out, the unexpected urge stemming from the same place as the need to hide away in a mountain of blankets did.

"Come. We go home now."

Home.

The repeated sentiment comes from Zuk, his silent communication sliding into my thoughts with such clarity I sob again.

Oktan pulls me downward, toward darkness and away from the only solace left in my life. I struggle against him, reaching up toward the sun.

"No. Don't make me go down there."

Yes. Home.

"No! Please!"

Teeth flash across my vision as Zuk crowds us, his impatience snapping through our bond.

Yes. Home.

"I hate the dark. Please, I can't go down there. I need sunlight!"

"Pale omega, we will protect you. Come."

Rage born of fear and some unknown source barrels over my misery and shoots daggers in the form of words from my mouth.

"I will make your life a living hell if you drag me down there."

Zuk's ominous chuckle sends a shiver down my spine while mockery fills Oktan's face. Time slows as he opens his mouth, both males surrounding me with their overpowering strength.

"Hell would be easier and safer than where we're taking you."

Author's note:

Sara, Oktan, and Zuk may swim away from the light of day, but I promise, darkness does not mean the end. While I must say goodbye for now, I plan to continue their story, so check out my links on the next page.

MORE FROM V.T.

We hope you enjoyed ***Of Tentacles and Fin*** by V.T. Bonds!

Jump into other knotty characters in the series *Depraved Monsters* and *Decadent Myths*.

Lured into the demon's lair.

In a nightmare I can't escape, I find true evil exists.

They have no mercy.

Can I survive their wicked savagery?

*This *Dark Omegaverse Romance* is not for the faint of heart. If *explicit scenes, violence, and D/s themes* offend you, please abstain. Proceed with caution.*

V.T. Bonds writes dark, action-packed romances full of overbearing alphas and strong-willed heroines.
Find her at: WWW.VTBONDS.WEBSITE

THE MONSTER UNDER MY BED

BY L.V. LANE

THE MONSTER UNDER MY BED

L.V. LANE

"Aren't you frightened living here all on your own?" my kindly neighbor, Mrs Johnson, asks. Our homes are tiny cottages nestled among the trees in the sleepy village of Tyne. Today she is visiting to drop off a basket full of cooking apples.

"No," I say, smiling as I take the laden basket from her hands. "I'm not afraid of that at all. Haven't I already told you? There's a monster living under my bed, and woe betide any stranger who would dare to harm his ward."

She laughs, and I laugh too. It is a fanciful tale, after all.

But as the door shuts on her cheery wave, I smile a different and secret smile.

I go about my day as usual. I bake an apple pie, I dust and sweep the floor, but all the while, I am thinking about the sweet and wicked monster who lives under my bed.

He has been there for as long as I can remember. When I was younger and my parents were still alive, he kept the bad things away. But now that I am older, he serves a very different purpose.

As night falls, I take my oil lamp and climb up the rickety wooden stairs to my bedroom, and placing the lamp on the nightstand, I ready myself for bed.

The sheets are cool as I slip between them. This is my favorite time of day, when I can fall into the other part of my life, one where monsters exist. I push my white nightgown all the way down to my knees and pull the covers up all the to my chin, enclosing myself inside.

Reaching over, I put out my lamp before swiftly tucking my hand back beneath the sheets.

As I lie in bed, my eyes adjust, tuning in to the darkness and shadows that seem to call me into their welcoming embrace. But they do not frighten me; the shadows comfort me here.

Tonight a sweet, achy tension is building inside. There is only one outlet for it, but I find I enjoy resisting the pull for a little while. I'm thinking about him, about him being under my bed. Knowing he is waiting brings a delectable type of thrill.

He knows the sign and what it means. We have

agreed on this long ago. Some nights I merely rest peacefully, knowing he is underneath my bed, and some nights I need a different kind of comfort from him. Tonight, as I gaze up at the darkened ceiling above my bed, I know I cannot resist.

Carefully I draw the covers back, just a little, just enough to slip my toes outside.

A loud thud and a screech come from beneath me, followed by a deep grinding vibration as he shifts, awakening and rousing himself to me and my needs.

Anticipation brings a flutter to my heart. I fidget, thinking about what is to come. My signal is an agreement that all power is given to him. It is always my choice how this starts, but it is his choice how it ends.

Another thud and a low rumble follow. I squeeze my thighs together as I sense him becoming sentient, becoming ever more aware of me.

I shift, pushing my whole foot out from under the covers. There will be no doubts now in my sweet monster's mind that his ward has needs.

I feel the faintest quickening, a featherlight touch across the arch of my foot. It is like a summer breeze stirring. I shiver, trying to anticipate what might come next, knowing that I will fail.

The whisper turns into the faint scrape of a claw. It runs the length of my arch all the way to my ankle.

Then another claw joins it, and then another, until a whole hand wraps all the way around.

I whimper softly. We have played this game many times, and I am conditioned to him and his ways.

Although my room is lost to shadows, I still see him as he morphs, and out of the blackness, a monster now looms. Towering, powerful, and covered in thick, dark fur—he is a beast in all ways.

He is about to do beastly things to me.

A great crackling, rumbly purr emanates from his chest. The hand wrapped around my ankle slides a little way up and down my calf. I groan, wanting more, wanting his hand to slide farther still.

He doesn't comply with my wishes, for my monster is not to be rushed.

Just knowing that he will do precisely the opposite of what I desire brings a clench deep inside my womb.

"Your needs are great tonight, my sweet little maiden," the monster says.

"Yes," I say. "Please, please do not make me wait. I cannot wait tonight."

My pleading only sees his purr shift to a husky laugh. "I foresee my maiden will spend a great deal of time begging tonight."

His hand moves from my ankle, and I whimper, missing his touch. He stands tall, straightening to his full height, head skimming the ceiling of my little country cottage. His chest heaves, broad shoulders rising as he draws in a deep breath. He moans, low and resonant, for my monster loves my scent.

His eyes shine in the darkness, meeting mine. There is nothing human about his features, shaggy fur, claws, and sharp teeth, but my fingers still clench as I anticipate petting the silken fur at the side of his snout.

My breath stutters as I feel the slightest tug on my covers before he draws them slowly off. He takes his time about this. My monster is never rushed. Slow increments see the heavy quilt drawn from my body, until finally it hits the floor with a soft thud. The cool night air finds my heated skin. My fidgeting has rucked up my nightgown a little, and between my thighs, I feel an unmistakable dampness as my body prepares for him.

"I can scent you, little maiden. Creaming for your monster, sweet pussy growing slick. Do you want your monster to taste you?"

"Yes," I say, arching up on the bed. My hands lower to my nightgown, and I dare to lift it a little way. He growls, and my hands immediately drop.

"No," he rumbles. "I will not attend to your needy little pussy yet. Tonight, I believe I will need to spend a great deal of time feasting on your pretty tits. Now open those silken ribbons at your throat and show me what is mine."

My hands shake as I reach for the ribbons at my

throat. The neat little bows come loose one by one until my nightgown is opened all the way to my waist. My chest rises and falls unsteadily, and I bite my lower lip to keep my whimpers in. If I do anything he perceives as intended to hurry him, he will assuredly go slower still.

"Good girl," he says. "Now part the material so that I may see your pretty tits."

My fingers shake so badly I can barely grasp the material. Fighting against my nature to rip it away, slowly, so slowly, I draw the edges apart. His deep purr is one of approval. The material feels unbearably coarse against my sensitive breasts, although it is the softest brush cotton I could find.

The air shifts as he lowers himself onto the bed, setting it creaking under his great weight. When he first awakens, his presence is like a tickling breeze. But as he solidifies into *being*, he has a delicious heaviness that I delight to feel pressing down over me.

Another deep, grumbly purr accompanies him nuzzling against the side of my breast. The fur tickles just before I feel the first lap of his coarse tongue. He lavishes attention all over the plump mound. Warm, wet, lashes of his tongue are followed by little nibbles that send butterflies to flight low in my belly. My fingers grasp on the bedding beside me, lest I break the spell and try to touch. Touching is forbidden until my monster gives me permission.

The faint scrape of a nail accompanies his ravishment of my breasts, but when I let out my groan of pleasure, he immediately stops.

"What a naughty little maiden," he teases in a raspy purr, snout tickling my skin as he moves upwards toward my throat. "Now your monster must start all over again."

And he does, driving me to the point of desperation one searing lick at a time, generously attends to both breasts, my throat, and the sensitive skin behind my ear until I am shuddering with delectable tension, desperate, and aching for his penetration.

A whimper escapes my tightly sealed lips as his nibbling takes him closer to the stiff peak that craves his touch. His rich, musky scent saturates my every breath, and as it draws into my lungs, it ignites a fluttering sensation in my belly, womb, breasts, and all the way to my heart.

My deep moan accompanies the first hot rasp of his tongue across my nipple. He pauses to nudge it with his nose before flicking his tongue over it again. It tightens, sensitive nerves flaring to life. Then he closes his beastly lips around it and gently sucks.

I twitch with pleasure. His head lifts, and dark eyes gaze down upon me through the gloom. He waits patiently as I gather my wits and remind myself to be still. Once I am settled, he begins his torment again.

On and on, it continues, drawing me higher,

lifting me up until the time between my twitching and his tending grows unbearably long. "Please," I plead. I do not mean to, for I know it will only worsen this torture, but I do, mumbled nonsense pouring from my lips, for I am insensible to everything but my needs.

"My maiden is very naughty tonight," my monster says, voice a husky drawl as he nibbles up the side of my throat.

Between my thighs is slick and ready for him to fill me, aching from the emptiness.

"Do you need your monster's cock?" he asks, his nose against my ear.

"Yes, please, yes. I need you. I'm so empty inside. Please fill me."

"My needs are also great tonight, little maiden. Do you feel my hands trembling?"

"Yes, yes I do."

"You know what happens when I am like this, little maiden. I fear I will have no option but to be quite rough with you." He nips gently at my throat, his claw-tipped thumb and fingers squeezing and tugging my distended nipple as if to emphasize this point.

"Please!"

"Hush, love. Let your monster have his pleasure. I must taste you before I can fill you deeply with my cock."

Another sharp tug upon my nipple draws a needy whimper from my lips.

"You need to be thoroughly prepared when I am in my most beastly and depraved of moods. I can scent your sweet pussy. My maiden is weeping encouragement for her monster to feast."

His snout lowers, nibbling a path down my body, pausing to tease my sore breasts, to squeeze, nibble, and lap them with his rough tongue. Finally he moves on, over my belly, hips, and belly again, before snuffling the nest of curls that hide my feminine place.

"Open up, little maiden, and let your monster have his first taste."

Legs thrusting open for him, I sob with joy as he takes a long lick.

He groans in echo, clawed fingers holding my thighs parted as he gently nibbles around the edges of the plump folds before taking another long, leisurely lick. Silken soft fur tickling where we touch sets all the sensations twisting joyously.

"Come for your monster," he rumbles against my pussy, making a vibration against the sensitive skin. A rough thumb strums back and forth against my swollen clit. "Give me more of your sweet body's offering. I will need to feast here for some time before I can be certain you are ready for the rough coupling that will follow."

I come apart, gasping, panting, feeling a great

gush eject from my body, soaking the fur around his snout as he greedily eats me out.

He growls his approval, easing the pressure of his thumb on my sensitive clit, and working his thick, sinuous tongue deeply into my pussy. My fingers bury into the soft fur at the side of his head, thighs straining to part farther to better provide access for his broad shoulders so that he might more easily pleasure me.

His thumb begins to move roughly against my clit again just as his thick tongue goes rigid and thrusts in and out of my slick pussy.

Another climax tears through me, my fingers fisting his thick fur, hips lifting, seeking more of this heady, rapturous torment.

I lose myself in the cycling pleasure, surrendering fully to the monster who lives under my bed and who ravishes me under the cover of darkness.

"Please," I beg again. "Please, I need to feel you inside." Desperation manifests in a desire for the connection that only comes when we are fully joined.

His head lifts, long tongue lapping the stickiness from his snout.

I lie panting, gazing up at the monster who commands both my body and my heart.

"Sweet maiden," he says. Rising, he cups my cheek in one huge hand. "I am going to ruin your perfect little pussy tonight."

I tremble before him. There is a different edge to him tonight.

His hands often tremble, but tonight they visibly shake.

My pretty nightgown is tugged up and off my body and tossed to the floor. As he braces over me, his great size dwarfs mine, bringing a familiar frisson of fear. Between his thighs, his beastly cock jerks, thicker than my forearm, the bright red tip emerging from its silken, lightly furred sheath.

My mouth waters.

"May I?" I ask, tearing my eyes from his monstrous cock to meet his monstrous gaze.

He nods, and my heart soars upon hearing this concession he gives rarely. Rising onto my knees, I gently close my small hands around his great girth.

"Goddess," I whisper as I carefully work his thick sheath back, exposing the bright, throbbing length of his cock. He is weeping pre-cum and is slick under my palms. Seeing it this close, handling it, makes my pussy clench with both fear and arousal. He has claimed me many times, yet I still wonder at how this powerful monster can join intimately with me.

Lowering my lips, I lap at his weeping slit, pumping, encouraging him to gift me more of his delicious taste.

One clawed hand gathers up my long hair,

holding it up and out of the way so that he can better see how I worship him.

"That's my good little maiden," he rumbles. "You are greedy for my cock and cum. I shouldn't let you take too much, but the feel of your precious little tongue greedily lapping is a heaven-sent test to my resolve. Try and suck the tip if you can, my love."

He lets out a low groan of pleasure as I do exactly that, jaw aching with the stain of even taking the very tip, but made determined by the growls of joy coming from my monster. My hands work up and down the hot, ridged flesh of his cock, all the way to the root and back to the tip, the thick knot near the base beginning to swell under my touch.

My belly tightens and my womb clenches, and then I am being drawn off, confused, licking the remnants from my lips and stuffing fingers into my mouth as he tumbles me onto my back.

He makes a tutting noise as he gently pulls my fingers from my mouth. "My greedy little maiden," he reproves, although I can hear the smile in his voice. "You have already coaxed my knot, and it will be a struggle for your naughty pussy to take. I have already told you of my great needs. There is no hope now but for me to take you very roughly indeed."

Every word is terrifying in its potency to arouse. I want him to ruin my pussy. I want the achy pain, and fear that envelops me as I wonder if he will break me with his monstrous cock.

Wrists captured within one clawed fist are pinned above me against the soft bedding. With a devious gleam in his beautiful eyes, he takes his great cock in hand and nudges the slick entrance to my pussy. My chest heaves unsteadily as the tip slowly breaches, forcing my muscles to give as the pressure rises.

I whimper and twitch, trying to find a position that eases the pressure. None do. His hand shifts to my waist, pinning me when I find it impossible to be still. I wanted this, yet now that the moment is bearing down upon me one thick inch at a time, my fear wars with a determination that I have done this before and that I can take all of him.

"Goodness!" I pant, writhing against his hold, finding it impossible to keep still, yet having nowhere to go.

"Can you feel that, my sweet maiden?" he demands as he saws his thick cock shallowly in and out. "All the ridges are already inflamed. You have coaxed your monster with your naughty tongue halfway into a rut."

He thrusts deeper suddenly, and I squeal, my nerves flaring to life and muscles straining in protest.

He growls when I try to buck him, pinning me more securely, plunging even deeper, opening me as he lowers his lips to nuzzle the side of my throat. One arm slides under me, bracing around my waist, pinning me absolutely still as he begins to rut.

My cries turn guttural, and my pussy gives under his sudden savagery. He growls, making the bed creak and rock as he deepens his strokes. The smaller ridges along his shaft flutter in and out, and the thick swelling of his greater knot bumps against my entrance with every firm slap of meeting flesh.

"Open up, little maiden," he growls into my ear.

"I can't!" My fingers clench into his soft fur at the scruff of his neck. He is bigger, harder, and barely restrained brutality as he powers into me, forcing my smaller, softer body to give.

Teeth nip against my throat before he growls and suddenly pulls out.

I blink up at him through the darkness, confused, bereft of his glorious cock.

There is a wicked glint in my monster's eyes as he shifts back onto his knees. "I told you my needs were great tonight, that I would let my most bestial side out."

I shake my head, realizing what he wants. Fear—genuine fear—rips through me.

"Please, it is too deep that way."

White teeth flash before I am tumbled onto my front. Hips in his hands, I am dragged backward, his cock snagging the entrance of my slick pussy before slamming deep.

"Munnnnn!" Face mashed against the bedding, my mumbled complaints turn into harsh moans as the pad of one rough finger finds my clit and begins to strum.

And there I hang, knees dangling as I am slammed on and off his monstrous cock. Heavy thrusts take him deeper, his knot slipping in and out of my pussy, stretching me, sending new sensations spiraling through me.

My pussy flutters. I can feel its terrible openness as he powers into me. Inner muscles, utterly spent under the savagery of the coupling, have no choice but to give. Sweat bathes my body as wet slaps give an indication of how he ruins me.

Then I am plummeting into rapture, pussy spasming, his thrusts invading even further as he forces his swelling knot in and out. He is harder, thicker, and deeper than he has ever been, and I the helpless human offering with which he slakes his lust.

"Take all of me, little maiden," he says, voice a raspy whisper.

Darkness comes for me as he squeezes his great hand around my throat. But it only rushes the sensations through me twice as fast.

"Give your monster what he needs," he growls. My pussy squeezes in obedience to his command, feeling the great girth of his knot slip inside one last time and hold. "That's it, my sweet little maiden. Give yourself to your monster."

The welcoming darkness pulls me in even as my body convulses into an orgasm that shatters my very soul. I twitch, fighting the need for air as all my thoughts converge on the rippling climax. Pleasure, so much pleasure—dark pleasure—skittering, blissful pleasure.

Then the suffocating pressure lifts, and the sensations spark twice as brightly.

White-hot ecstasy dances across the surface of my skin. Inside, so deep, I feel the first hot jets of his cum. His roar of release is loud enough to make the walls and floor vibrate. I hang limp, cheek mashed to the bedding, body racked by heady shudders as my monster fills me all up. I want more of him; I always want more.

Gusty breaths follow as we remain locked together, my pussy clenching in little aftershocks, his hands now gentle as they hold me.

Once his knot softens and we can move, I cling to him, nestling within the cage of his arms, cheek to the soft fur of his chest as his hands roam over my back and ass. A deep, resonant purr emanates from his chest, and I cling harder, weeping from the intensity of what we have shared.

When my tears peter out, he eases away enough to place a finger under my chin and tip it so that he might see my face.

"What is it, love?" he asks.

"I—I don't want you to go again," I say. "I know that you must—that you are the monster who lives under my bed, and that you cannot possibly stay—

but I don't want you to go. I want you to stay so badly. I am terrified to sleep, for when I do, you always fade away."

I sob harder again. My body is exhausted, my pussy a good kind of sore from his attention, yet I want more. I want him inside me again, filling this emptiness.

Lowering my head, I burrow into the fur of his chest, small hands clinging. "I want you again. I need you."

Lips brush against my temple before he rolls onto his back, encouraging me to climb over him. "Take, my love. Take me however you want and need. I am here for you, always, in whatever way you require."

His words seem to have another meaning, a potency that my sorrow-ravaged mind cannot quite grasp. But I also need to feel him inside me, and I grasp his thick cock, sobbing with joy as I battle to sink down onto it.

"Careful, love," he rumbles. Taking my hips in his big hands, he helps me, doing much of the work, yet allowing me to decide on the pace and depth of our coupling.

Hands braced against the firm muscles of his chest, I embrace the achy pleasure as sore inner muscles give and I ride his monstrous cock. "More," I say. "Please, I need more."

With a growl of satisfaction, he begins to slam up into me even as he holds my hips.

"Yes!"

This feels different. Always it is my choice how this begins, but always it is his choice how it ends. Only today, it feels like all of it is mine. Today the beginning, and now the end, is by my design.

My love for him, that once-innocent love which changed over time into passion and desire, blazes within my chest. My climax sideswipes me out of nowhere in hot waves, my pussy convulsing around his great cock and knot, sapping the last of my energy as he follows me into rapture.

I am spent after, collapsing over him. I am tired, and although I try desperately to cling to consciousness lest he disappear, exhaustion drags me into a fitful sleep.

I AWAKE to a sensation of discord. Something tickles my nose, and I shift, groaning when I find my thighs spread wide around a great body... a great furry body.

"Uh? Oh! Ow!"

"What ails you, tiny maiden?" a gruff voice demands. Strong, fur-covered arms tighten around me.

My pains are momentarily overwritten by the

realization that daylight streams through the window... and *he* is still here.

I blink at my monster in wonder, a monster I am sprawled over.

A monster I have never seen in daylight.

His broad snout tugs up in what I believe to be a grin.

"Oh!" I say, cupping the side of his muzzle. Its softness is familiar, but I am seeing the multi-faceted shades of brown in his fur for the very first time. "You are so beautiful!"

"I am?" he asks, incredulous. His eyes, like his fur, are a tawny golden brown. They are the most wondrous eyes I have ever seen, and they seem to sparkle in the morning light.

"Yes!" I say, sobbing as I throw my arms around his neck, burying my nose into his soft fur and clinging like he might be snatched away. "How? How are you here?"

"Foolish little maiden. Don't you know you could keep me with you, were it only what you truly desired?"

"No! Oh, please say you will never go away again! I love you. I love you so much, my sweet monster who has cared for me all my life."

"I will not," he says. "You have willed me into your life, and you cannot will me away again. We are bonded. I too have loved you your whole life, first as an innocent child who needed to feel safe in the darkest hours of the night, and later as a woman with your loving, giving ways. Now you must be burdened with a monster who will not fit under your bed for the rest of your life."

I giggle, lifting my head and inspecting my monster once again, leaning up—with a wince, for I am very sore—as I take all of him in.

His eyes narrow in a way I have never witnessed before. "You are sore?" he demands.

"I... A little," I say, blushing and unexpectedly feeling very shy.

Suddenly, I am tipped onto my back.

"What—What are you doing?" I ask nervously, for he is lifting his great monster body from my bed, setting it creaking and groaning and lowering his snout between my thighs.

He pauses to glance up, lips tugging in what I am coming to understand is his smile.

"Don't you know, my sweet maiden? Can't you guess?"

I shake my head, blushing to the roots of my hair, and a little nervous because I can now fully see this magnificent monster who pauses with his snout inches from my sore pussy.

"Allow me to demonstrate," he rumbles. "We monsters have a reputation for ruining needy pussies, but we also have the best cures to make them all better again."

Lowering his mouth, he buries it in my hot, wet, swollen pussy... and gently laps.

"Goddess," I mumble, fingers fisting his soft fur as he takes the soreness away one heavenly lick at a time. "Please tell me you shall do this every day."

"Every day," he promises in a husky rasp against my pussy, which is no longer sore and is instead needy again. "I shall worship your sweet body whenever my sweet maiden desires."

The End.

MORE FROM L.V.

We hope you enjoyed ***The Monster Under My Bed*** by L.V. Lane!

Continue the world of *Coveted Prey* with Book One, *Prey: A Fantasy Reverse Harem*.

Prey is a fantasy reverse harem omegaverse with three stern alphas, an alpha wolf-shifter, and their stubborn omega prey.

L.V. Lane writes mostly sci-fi and fantasy romance that follows a theme... Dominant alphas, sweet, sassy, bratty heroines who give their alphas a hard time, high heat, omegaverse or alien or enhanced human in some way!

WWW.AUTHORLVLANE.COM

MY MONSTER

BY LEANN RYANS

MY MONSTER

LEANN RYANS

I WAS ALONE in the darkness.

Or I thought I was.

The small noises that reached me could be explained away. A rat scurrying down the tunnel beyond. The wind whipping through openings in the caves.

I'd chosen what I thought was the most secure cavern to create my nest. It wasn't the deepest, I hadn't been able to reach an end to the cave system, but it was off a side tunnel where I thought I wouldn't be found.

Not that it seemed like there was anyone to find me. I knew my home village wasn't the only one in these mountains, but I hadn't seen a single person since the night I'd ran away.

My father's death had left me with no protection. On the cusp of my first heat, I was being fought over by the alphas before his body had even cooled.

And I wouldn't let myself be claimed by the ones that seemed likely to win.

Murderous slobs. Little better than filthy animals. Even the monsters they told stories of would be a better choice than any of them.

But that left me going into heat alone in the mountains.

Stumbling across the cave had seemed to be a blessing, and finding the system beyond was more than I could have hoped for. Despite not encountering anyone during my trek, I hadn't wanted to be exposed while I was vulnerable. The caves would keep my scent from spreading on the wind and drawing in any alpha close enough to be affected by my pheromones.

I tossed restlessly on my meager pile of rushes. The cramps were already ripping at my middle when I found my hiding place, so I hadn't had much time to prepare. The armful of sweet grass I hadn't been able to resist as I made my way through the woods wasn't enough to cushion the hard stone below me. Even adding my cloak overtop it didn't make the unforgiving surface any more pleasant.

A whine escaped as I thought of my bed. The piles of pillows and blankets I'd hoarded over the years in preparation. They would have been added to the bedding provided by the alpha my father chose for me, yet even he hadn't found anyone in our village worthy of an omega bride. He'd planned to take us to a new village with better prospects, but when the others found out, they'd killed him.

Tears built, spilling over and running down my grubby cheeks, but my mind couldn't focus on grief with lava burning through my veins. My middle tightened, lungs locking as another wave of pain spread from my core. Fresh slick spilled over my thighs, but I was beyond the point of caring about my sorry state.

A soft sob left me as the cramp passed, eyes blinking open in a vain effort to find distraction. Eyes opened or closed, there was no difference in what I could see. Perhaps that was why the small sounds I heard kept catching my attention.

A scuff pulled my head to the left. I'd turned too many times to know which direction I faced or where the tunnel entrance was, but instincts said the sound came from beyond my little cave.

Ears straining to catch more noise, I held my breath as I waited. My heart was racing in my chest, fluttering as fissions of fear streaked through me.

Had I been found?

I'd done my best to cover my tracks as I left the village. Sticking to the hard path until I reached the stream, then wading through it until my feet were so numb I could no longer feel them. Even when I left the water I was careful to climb out over a fall of rocks so I wouldn't leave any traces. I'd camped without a fire, eating the food I'd stuffed in the one bag I'd brought with me as I huddled beneath my cloak, yet visions of the alphas from the village bursting into my cave filled my head.

My core clenched again, and I had to swallow back a cry of pain. Lips pinched together, I trembled through the building pressure until another gush of fluid escaped between my legs.

The fabric beneath me was soaked, the sweet smell of slick overpowering the aroma released by the grass. My body went limp when the cramp passed, leaving me panting as I tried to prepare for the next. They would continue until my heat was over or I was knotted by an alpha. Without their potent seed to soothe the burning demand of my womb, it was going to be a rough few days.

My head lolled and my breathing eased as I let my mind drift again. I already felt weak from days of travel coupled with the loss of fluid, but I couldn't search for water in my state. I had a little left in my waterskin, but I had to save it for after my heat broke.

If I lasted that long.

Another scrape sounded beyond my little bubble, but I was too tired to lift my head and look for the source. It was all in vain anyway when I was enveloped in darkness. I couldn't even see the hand at the end of my arm.

Turning to try to get comfortable, another whine

slipped through my control, the soft sound seeming loud as it echoed around me. I had no idea what else could be living in the cave system I'd found, I could only hope whatever it was would be scared away from the scent of human. It wouldn't be long before I was in no state to defend myself.

As I fell deeper into the daze of my encroaching cycle, the sounds outside my tiny cave became more frequent. The steady scraping had a rhythmic pattern, one I knew I should recognize, but my brain refused to focus on anything outside the demands of my own body. The heat building beneath my skin, the irritation of the restrictive dress twisting around me with each change of position, the building pressure in my womb, and the pulsing throb of need between my thighs.

Rolling over again, the abrasive brush of my coarse dress across my tightened nipples became too much. I rose to my knees, tugging it off with a growl and tossing it somewhere beyond the bounds of my nest. It didn't matter that I'd struggle to find it once my cycle passed, only that the offending material was beyond my current reach.

Cool air brushed across my sensitive flesh, bringing a sigh to my lips as I let myself sit back on my heels. There was a new scent on the breeze that played through my cave, something musky and rich and mouthwatering, but I didn't know where it came from. It teased my senses, prickling the hairs on the back of my neck, and bringing a fresh surge of slick from my core.

I couldn't resist the need for release any longer.

My hand slipped between my thighs even as shame filled my cheeks. I knew it was natural for omegas to desire sex during their cycle, but I'd never touched myself before, and the thought of filling myself with my own fingers seemed somehow naughtier than submitting to a male.

My fingertips slipped through the fluids coating my feminine folds, seeking something to ease the ache. A gasp ripped from my lips as they passed over a small bump at the top of my opening, sensations spiking through my middle and making me freeze.

A new throb began in the little bundle I'd found, demanding I touch it again. I moved to my back as I switched between circling the little nub and brushing over the top of it, tension building in my belly but refusing to release. My head tossed from side to side, tears leaving burning tracks on my face as I begged my body for the relief it refused to find.

I didn't realize I was crying out loud until a sudden noise froze the sounds in my throat. My body went on alert, stilling as my ears strained to find the source of whatever startled me. The scent I'd noticed earlier had grown stronger, coating my tongue in the heady aroma that made me think of nothing more than *male*.

"Don't let me interrupt you, little omega. I was enjoying the show."

The gruff voice echoed through the darkness, ripping a gasp from me as I scrambled away from the sound. My entire body throbbed with denied need as I crouched and searched desperately for the source. A small part of my brain recognized I was in danger, but my body only responded by releasing more slick to roll down my thighs, like that would save me.

The next cramp threatened to tear my body in half, the muscles in my middle rippling and forcing me into a ball of misery at the edge of my nest. Whoever was in the cave with me hadn't been a voice I recognized, and I was beyond the point of being able to run.

"Please..."

It was the only word I could force past trembling lips, and even I didn't know what I was asking for. Part of me demanded I send the male away while another part wanted me to roll over and present. The deepness of the voice and the scent surrounding me left no question that the speaker was an alpha.

"Please what, little one? Do you need help?"

A whimper was my only response. With the pheromones of the male taking effect in my brain, the cramps had become non-stop, one rolling in on the heels of the last, leaving me breathless and crying into the thin grass covering the stone. My core clenched over and over, demanding to be filled with thick alpha cock.

I heard the same scraping sound as before coming closer, stopping at the edge of the little depression I'd claimed for my heat. A low growl left my throat before I could think, but it was only met with a chuckle from the hulking male I could sense at the edge of my space.

"Temper, temper. I'm only offering to give you what you need."

There was a strange accent to the words the male spoke, but they were clear enough to understand. Despite the delicious scent rolling off him and the demands of my body, it was instinct to protect my nest, even as pitiful as it was.

There still wasn't any light in the cave, but the alpha's presence was enough for my eyes to lock on to where I assumed he stood. The sense of motion caused me to flinch further away but there were no more scraping footsteps, and nothing touched me.

Another harsh cramp pulled my focus back to myself, the desire between my thighs growing more desperate with each breath of the male's musk. My hand slipped to my core again without conscious thought, two fingers dipping into my entrance to try to ease the pain, but only succeeding in making me more miserable.

I wasn't going to make it for days like this. It was torture.

I pushed another finger into my opening, ignoring the alpha's presence and thrusting in and out desperately. Something had to give, and I was scared it would be me giving into the male lurking so close.

A soft moan escaped my throat as my knuckles stretched my entrance, but it wasn't enough. I needed more.

"Poor omega. I have what your body craves."

I snarled towards the male, turning so my back was to where the voice originated. It came from lower than it had before and I could picture him crouching on the edge of my nest, watching as I tried to ease the ache. Waiting for the inevitable.

His scent was divine. There was a saltiness to it now that spoke of virility. That called to the animal parts of me and told me this was a male in his prime. A male worth submitting to.

I panted as my fingers worked. Free hand braced against the stone edge of my wallow, I tried to ride my thrusting digits, but it couldn't provide the stretch or the friction my nature demanded. Even adding my little finger to the other three did nothing.

Time had no meaning in the desperate daze I'd fallen into. It could have been hours or days or mere seconds that passed in my search for relief before I finally collapsed with a sob.

I'd almost forgotten about the male perched at the side of my nest until he spoke again.

"Give in little one. Let me soothe your pain."

"I will submit to no man."

My snarled words echoed back to me even as a chuckle rumbled through the cave.

"Well, I am no man."

It was divine agony watching the little omega and waiting for her to give in to the inevitable. She'd already lasted longer than I'd expected.

It was pure luck that she'd ended up in the set of caves I claimed as my own and not in one of the many others in the area. If I hadn't scented her at the entrance and followed her trail I still could have lost the opportunity to claim her as my own.

And I *would* claim her. The little omega was mine, she just didn't know it yet. I'd paced outside the cavern she'd chosen until I was sure she was too far gone to run before moving inside and announcing my presence.

I chuckled again at the gasp that escaped her. There was no way she hadn't heard the stories. The tales of monsters living in the mountains, hunting the woods, killing the villagers who strayed too far.

They were exaggerated, of course. Not the monster part, that was true enough. By human standards my kind were certainly monstrous with fur, claws, fangs, and horns, but we rarely killed villagers unless they gave us reason to.

"Wh—what do you mean?"

Her voice was a breathy gasp, her fingers stilling at my announcement as a hint of fear crept back into the sweet scent of her. Her eyes searched the area around me, too weak to see through the darkness as I could.

"You know what am, omega. You knew the minute I stepped into the cave. Your body warned you even before, yet your heat made you stay because you know I can ease the pain."

I shifted from the crouch I'd held since approaching her nest, moving to kneel right on the edge of the depression. It was a pathetic nest, but it was likely the best she'd been able to do in her circumstances. It was clear she came from one of the villages and didn't have the knowledge to be on her own in the wild. My curiosity about how she got her could wait though.

She whimpered, one hand clutching her belly as the other moved with unconscious thought between her thighs. The scent of slick drenched the cave, drowning me in the pheromones of a breedable female.

My cock leaked more fluid in response, the tangy scent mingling with hers and trying to entice the human closer. I could see her nostrils flaring, her eyes locking on me despite her inability to see.

She didn't need sight to know where relief waited. It was better this way. It would be easier for her to accept me if she couldn't see how different I was.

My toes flexed, claws scraping the stone beneath me and causing her breathing to stutter.

"Monster."

The word was a mere whisper, but it still brought a smirk to my lips. I'd been called it enough times in my life for the sting to no longer affect me. It'd become something of a badge I proudly wore.

"You're right, human. I'm what you'd call a monster, though I've met enough humans who have earned the title more than I have. What's more important at the moment is the other thing you should be calling me."

I watched her thighs clench and her hips lift instinctively. Monster or not, I was alpha, and she was omega. Her body yearned for mine the same way I was drawn to her.

"Alpha," she breathed.

My cock jerked, spitting a glob of seed onto the cloak she'd laid over the grass to cushion her nest. Fingers curling around my length, I pulled, bringing more of my offering spilling from the tip.

The little omega licked her lips, body leaning closer as she sniffed the air. Her dark hair shifted over her shoulders, hiding her lush tits from my view, but I held back the growl that threatened. I'd worked too hard to reach this point to scare her off now.

She turned until she faced me, still braced on one hand with the other buried between her legs, her neck stretched toward where I rested outside the bounds of her nest. As wretched as it was, it was still her sacred place, and I wouldn't invade without invitation.

Her knees shuffled, moving her closer until the hand guiding her slid into the seed on her cloak. She froze, body going stiff before she lifted her fingers to her nose.

I couldn't stop the groan that left me as her tongue extended to lap up my offering, my erection jerking in jealousy. I was leaking so much it ran down my shaft to matt the fur covering my balls and thighs, my knot already threatening to swell.

After the first tentative taste the little omega sucked her fingers clean, scooping up the rest of what was on the cloak before letting out a whine of disappointment.

"There's more where that came from. Just come a little closer."

I could reach her if I stretched out my arm, but I wanted her to come to me. I needed her to be the one to initiate and bring me into her nest.

Then I'd take what I'd been waiting so long for.

Omegas were rare and jealously guarded. I'd

never thought to find one, much less one as perfect as the little human.

I held my breath as she hesitated. I was reaching my limit, and if the omega didn't give in soon I wasn't sure I'd be able to continue holding back.

She saved me from that thought as she went down to all fours, crawling closer. Quiet whimpers escaped her throat, but I pushed out a purr to reassure her and guide her to me. I could tell when she was close enough to feel the heat from my body since she paused and sat back on her heels once again, and it was a fight to keep my purr from dipping into a growl.

Small hands lifted, extended toward me. I could see her fingers trembling as she reached.

Her left hand connected with my hip, the right a little lower, sinking into the fur on my thighs.

I SQUEAKED and my fingers clenched, some tangling in hair while the others raked the smooth skin of his lower abdomen. Despite the fear mingling with the heat in my blood, I didn't pull away, his scent and the purr thrumming from his chest keeping me in a daze.

"Good girl. You can touch me. Find what you want."

The words were all the reminder and permission I needed.

The taste of his seed still coated my tongue. There was nothing else it could have been, the salty tang that smelled of musk and virility. I don't know what prompted me to lick my fingers when they came in contact with the sticky goop, but now I needed more.

My right hand moved first, creeping up the thickly muscled thigh. The hair was too dense to call anything other than fur. It was about as long as the tip of my finger, from the point to the first knuckle, and was surprisingly soft.

My left palm rested on his hip bone. The fur was thinner and gave way to smooth skin where my fingers rubbed back and forth. I could feel the muscle rippling under my touch, the power coiled within the male poised over me enough to make my whole body tremble.

A monster. I was touching a monster.

I found his heavy sac first. Round and firm and far larger than I'd have guessed. I'd seen men naked before, even caught glimpses of alphas rutting the tavern wench in the barn, but they hadn't looked as big as the male under my hands.

Licking dry lips, I let my fingers wander upward, tracing over his balls to the hard shaft above. While his sac had been densely furred like his leg, the hair tapered away to silky skin stretched tight over his pulsing length.

The moan that left me was wanton. Palm coated

in his fluids, it slipped easily over ridges, up to the flared head of his penis, more cream coating my fingers as he twitched in my hold. I couldn't enclose the whole thing in my grip, he was so thick, and my core gave a needy spasm at the thought of being impaled on it.

But first I needed another taste.

My nose guided me to where my hand circled beneath the edge of his tip, tongue slipping out to steal another taste of his offering. I moaned again, lapping up his fluids as my hand worked to milk more from his shaft.

My other dropped to join it as I opened my mouth and took his head inside. The flavor of him was unlike anything I'd ever tried. Salty, earthy, and robust, I felt like I'd waste away if I didn't get more of it.

My teeth scraped against his flesh as I tried to take more of him into my mouth. His cock kicked and a hand cupped the back of my head before gathering my locks in its hold.

"Easy, omega. I'll give you what you need."

That rough, rumbly voice caused a flutter in my core. My cramps had eased with the first taste of his seed on my fingers, but it wasn't enough to see them finished.

I needed more of it. I needed to swallow him down. Feel my stomach bulge with his release.

I tried to force myself further down his shaft but

the hand in my hair pulled me back. I gasped as my scalp prickled but I didn't stop jerking his length.

"Now."

I had no idea where the demanding tone came from. The fact that he was a monster didn't matter, only that he could ease the pain I'd suffered through for hours.

Another chuckle was the only response he gave before releasing my hair to tumble against my back.

"Have it your way then."

The words held the threat of more than I could handle, but I was too lost in need to care. Large hands cradled the sides of my head a moment later, palms on my cheeks and long fingers reaching to the back of my skull. The tiny pricks of pain on my scalp had to be caused by claws, but instead of frightening me like that should, my body shuddered at the thought of him raking them over my breasts and across the insides of my thighs.

The alpha held my head still as his hips began to pump. Until that moment he hadn't moved, letting me have my way with him, but now he'd taken over.

My hands moved to his thighs, instinctively trying to slow him and hold him back, but my strength was nothing compared to his.

He used me, fucking my mouth and forcing me down until my jaw was stretched as wide as it could go. The head of his cock popped into my throat, blocking my air, and still he used me.

Just when I was growing dizzy with the need to breathe, he pulled back. My chest inflated with a ragged gasp before he was filling my throat again.

I knew I should be terrified. I should be worried that he'd go too far. But all I could think about was tasting more of his seed as he spilled in my mouth.

I kept my lips firm around him, tongue laving the underside of his shaft as he pumped. His purr had dropped an octave, on the edge of being a growl that had my nipples tightened to painful points and slick running down my thighs in a constant stream. I could hear him panting above me, the sounds of his enjoyment building the fire burning in my core.

"Get ready, little one. Just a bit more."

His voice was a groan like he was in pain. The massive thighs beneath my palms trembled, twitching as his thrusts grew erratic.

He pulled back and allowed me to suck in another desperate breath before the first spray coated my tongue. I swallowed eagerly as he filled my mouth with pulse after pulse of his seed, the taste of him sending my eyes rolling back in my head.

He gripped my hair with one hand again as the other moved to stroke his shaft, just the head remaining in my mouth. As the flood slowed he pulled out, using his hold on my hair to bow me backwards and send the last of his release spraying over my body.

I licked my lips to get every drop I could reach as

the hand not holding me moved to rub his spend into my skin. Across my breasts and down my belly, all the way to my mons, the monster smeared me with the scent of him, sending a shiver down my spine.

Belly full, the need to taste him sated, my core still throbbed in demand.

I needed him to fill me. Fuck me. Soothe the incessant need.

When he was done massaging his seed into my skin he pulled me against his chest, massive arm wrapping around my back so his hand could knead my bottom. His still hard cock nestled between my legs and the tips of his claws dug into my flesh, but there was no pain.

Hands lifting to grip his shoulders, I rubbed myself against him, the hair that began again on his chest abrading my nipples and sending zings of sensation straight to my clit. The skin of his belly was smooth and hair-free except for a thin stripe that connected the hair on his chest to the hair sprouting around his manhood, but the rest of him seemed covered in the same dense fur.

Warm breath ghosted over the top of my shoulder as his head dipped. An abrasive tongue licked the side of my neck, bringing goosebumps to the surface as I shuddered.

The head next to mine was not shaped like a human. It was larger, rounded, and the tongue was far too big to fit in a human mouth.

I raised my hands to feel him since I couldn't rely on my eyes, but the alpha spun me around before I could touch his face.

"Not yet, little human. You're not ready for that."

Fresh fear bloomed in my chest but it was drowned out by the lust still coursing through my veins. A part of me wondered how scary he could really be, while another didn't care as long as he used the thickness now prodding my bottom to end my heat.

My back arched as one of his hands palmed my breast, fingers pinching my nipple and pulling a gasp from my throat. He rocked his hips, cock dragging through the cleft of my ass and causing my core to clench in demand.

"In me."

I wiggled my hips, urging him to delve between my folds, but those two words were all I could get past my lips. Thinking was too hard, I only wanted to feel.

His chuckle vibrated through my back, the hand not playing with my breasts sliding down my belly to circle my throbbing clit.

"You haven't invited me into your nest yet, and I still need a taste."

A spasm rocked through me at the thought of the rough tongue I'd felt on my neck licking the delicate flesh between my thighs. Slick splattered the floor beneath my knees as I whimpered.

"Yes."

I wiggled, the alpha releasing me so I could shuffle forward and lean down to press my chest to my cloak, ass high. The sound that left him was too deep to be a purr, making my body shudder as I moaned.

"Do you accept me, omega? Do you want me in your nest?"

The words sounded formal, but I was too lost to think about what he was asking. Nodding into the floor, I gasped out another, "Yes."

He was on me in a second, calloused hands gripping my thighs to hold me in place as his tongue dipped into my folds. I squealed with the first swipe, the sensation too intense, and tried to pull away.

The alpha didn't let me move. Lick after lick he drove me higher, my body coiling tighter, until the tension inside finally snapped.

Light exploded behind my eyelids as I cried out. My legs thrashed, trying to kick the male away from my exposed core when he didn't relent. His tongue thrust into my entrance, further than my mind could accept as he lapped up my release with little grumbles of pleasure.

When he finally moved away from my core my body was a puddle of melted flesh. Limp and weak,

I'd have collapsed to the ground if he'd released my hips, but he wasn't giving me a chance to recover.

A smooth, scalding tip pressed to my opening. He didn't give me a chance to protest, sinking in with steady pressure even as my body tried to clench and keep him out.

"Relax, little one. Let me in."

I could tell the words came from between clenched teeth, the growl in them barely restrained. It was instinct to try to escape his invasion, but my wiggling did nothing more than move the stiffness around inside me as it advanced, hitting things along my walls that made my legs go weak once again.

I was a panting, whiny mess long before he'd buried his full length inside me. Stretched wide around the length of him, I gave a hiccupping sob at the thought that I'd been begging to be stretched like this only a short time ago, and now I was begging him to stop.

"Just a little more."

His arm slipped around my hip, a finger moving to rub my clit as he pulled back. The relief was short lived as he thrust himself forward again, forcing more of his cock inside. His manipulation of my little bud had fresh slick seeping past his intrusion, and with the next push he finally seated himself to the base.

It burned.

I was stretched so wide it felt like I was splitting open. I could feel the head of his cock crammed against my back wall, leaving me full and uncomfortable as his hips finally stilled.

"Good girl. That's it."

The hand holding my hip flexed as the other continued rubbing between my legs. The longer he held still the more the pain of his invasion lessened and my muscles slowly relaxed, giving in to the pleasure building from his fingers. When he finally pulled his length back out, all I wanted was for him to fill me again.

And he did.

Over and over the monster's cock plunged into me, battering my womb as I cried out. His fingers never stopped working my little nub, the pressure and tension building inside me so much stronger than the first time I was sure I'd die if it didn't release.

The swelling of his knot brought back the burning pain at my entrance, but I was too close to completion for it to distract me. The stretch ached as he pulled it out of my opening and forced it back in, each second seeing it thicken further. When a hand reached up to gather my hair and pull it to one side, the teeth that scraped over my neck was the final straw.

Screaming, my core spasmed around the thick cock lodged in my channel. Even his knot locking behind my pubic bone and the sharp teeth piercing my shoulder couldn't bring me down from the high he'd forced me to.

My entire body trembled with sensation, every place his body touched mine feeling electrified as he continued to grind himself inside me. The first pulse of his seed was like lava being sprayed against my womb, the heat searing me from the inside as tears tracked down my cheeks.

As my orgasm eased and the quaking of my limbs stilled, the pain came back full force. My core throbbed, the alpha's knot stretching me more than a fist would have, but it wasn't until he pulled his teeth from my shoulder and licked the wound that the full force of what had happened hit me.

I'd been claimed by a monster. Some kind of beast I'd yet to see, covered in fur, but as intelligent as any person.

As he rolled us to the side and curled his larger body around mine, I tried to remember my fear, but the purr throbbing into my spine and the contentment I could feel unfurling inside me left me too relaxed to worry. The alpha had shown me more consideration by respecting the boundary of my nest than any male in my home village would have, and his actions clearly showed he wasn't the type of monster the stories made them out to be.

With nowhere else to go or family left to judge, why couldn't I give the monster a chance? A bond was for life and there was no way to break it outside the death of one of us. He'd already claimed me, so wouldn't it be better to give in to the pull of my instincts and accept my alpha?

The swelling of his knot eased as I laid in his arms and considered the way I felt. Being mated to a monster wasn't something I'd ever considered unless you labeled the murderous men who truly deserved it as monsters. As the alpha behind me stroked my sides and gently licked his mark, I decided what he looked like didn't matter. I could feel the goodness in him behind my breastbone, where a part of him had already taken up residence.

Twisting in his arms when his knot popped free, I ran my hands up his chest to his shoulders and wiggled myself higher. Searching the darkness, I gave up on trying to find his eyes and laid my cheek against his collarbone before repeating what he'd asked me earlier.

"I accept you, my alpha, and I want you in my nest. Always."

Turning my head, I opened my mouth wide and bit into the muscle on the side of his neck. Clawed hands tightened around me, my mate's gasp echoing in the chamber where I'd made my nest. With the first taste of his rich blood the bond between us bloomed, strengthening until I could feel his heart beating alongside mine, the joy and pride rushing through him to flood my body.

My purr rose to join his as I released, licking the

crescent that marked him as mine. I had no idea what the future held, but unlike my lonely trek away from my village, I now had someone to face it with. Someone whose loyalty and desire filled me with the knowledge that I'd never be scared or alone again.

My monster would protect me, now and always.

MORE FROM LEANN

We hope you enjoyed ***My Monster*** by Leann Ryans!

Did you enjoy the rustic feel of the story? If you'd like to read more like it, check out the *Alpha Barbarians* series beginning with *Raider's Treasure.*

As an omega, Lyric never had a choice in who she'd mate.

She was resigned to the man her father chose until the day warriors attacked her village, killing her father and her betrothed.

The leader plans to keep her for himself. He offers the others a choice… if she gives herself to him willingly.

But can she forgive what he did to her village?

Leann Ryans writes a variety of omegaverse stories that fall somewhere between soft and fluffy, and dark and depraved. If you enjoy tough heroes who are sweet in their own ways,

WWW.LEANNRYANS.COM

DEMON OF HER DREAMS

BY GODIVA GLENN

DEMON OF HER DREAMS

GODIVA GLENN

FARRAH SHIVERED on the windy balcony of her hotel room, scanning the sky for stars. High above the gaudy fluorescent signs and ambitious floodlights of the casinos, she made out a few twinkling constellations. A yawn broke over her as she wished on one of them.

She was exhausted. She couldn't remember the last time she'd experienced a decent night's rest, yet she fought her body's pull to go to bed. Sleep terrified her—or rather—the nightmare did. Each night, it grew darker and more desperate. And somehow, more real.

She pulled the knitted sleeves of her sweater over her hands, wrapping her chilled fingertips into the fabric. The cold had helped to keep her awake at first, but not so much now. She stepped back into the room and instantly warmed as she pulled the door shut behind her.

The hotel had been part of a desperate attempt to rid herself of the recurring nightmare, assuming that a vacation would free her of whatever stress was causing her turmoil. Three days in, it hadn't made a difference. The spa, the hot tub, the view—it didn't matter. The hotel held happy memories for her, but perhaps missing the source of that happiness only added fuel to the twisting chaos that found her the moment she slipped into the dream world. Everything here reminded her of Nathan, and when she'd booked the trip, that had seemed like a good idea. Now that she was here, it seemed like the worst idea possible.

She sat on the sofa and sank into the cushions, thinking of turning on a movie, something that would keep her up. She began to reach for the remote, but her hand didn't move.

Farrah stared at the remote and the glass coffee table it sat on. They faded from view as if the entire room was stretching away, placing them out of her reach. She looked at her hand, and as she studied it, she realized the room had dimmed, the lights above her fading into shadow. She swallowed and stood, feeling a familiar tingling at the back of her neck and inhaling an ominous, stale scent. She'd fallen asleep, and the nightmare had found her as swiftly as ever.

Claws dug lightly at her arms. She didn't have to

see them to know they were black extensions of his fingers, though sometimes everything would flicker and they wouldn't be claws, but normal fingertips, as if a man lurked within the demonic exterior.

A brief scrape—one not sharp enough to cut, but enough to send a shiver up her spine—made her heart thump in her ears. She jabbed one elbow back against his chest before the touch could turn into a hold and ran into the dark landscape of the nightmare.

She could barely see in front of herself. The nightmare realm was dark with sporadic flashes of orange and red, the light appearing in jagged streaks like lightning in a cloudy sky. In the distance were buildings, but they seemed to float away if she aimed for them. Instead she looked for smaller shadows along the ground, cast by the rubble of fallen structures.

Her foot caught on something and she stumbled. It couldn't have been a root—she'd never seen a tree or anything else living in this place—but she didn't look down or back to see what it may have been. She sucked in deep breaths of the hot, dusty air as she raced and searched for cover. The longer she could run, the shorter the nightmare would be. Once she'd gotten a fraction of rest in the outside world, she could break free.

A black swirl formed in front of her, blocking her vision. She turned from it, but it caught her. Hands pulled her back against a tall, muscular body, one she knew and feared. She struggled until the arms wrapped around her fully.

After nights of running and hiding, of seeing him only in brief glimpses, he'd finally caught her.

Moisture pressed to the side of her neck as he kissed her there and drew his tongue across her skin, tasting her. Farrah shivered, and a scream welled inside her, but didn't escape. She could try to scream and yell, but nothing ever came out. Whenever he appeared, it wasn't her dream anymore. She couldn't control it.

Tonight.

The word made her cold. He didn't speak, exactly; the hissing sound of his voice broadcasted directly into her brain. The nightmare never made sense, yet his single word held confidence. It was a promise, one she didn't want him to succeed in keeping.

Submit.

That word was a constant. Every chase, every night, all came down to his insistence that she submit. She never would.

He buried his face into the black, curly mass of her hair and inhaled so deeply she could hear it. When he exhaled, it tickled her scalp. He caressed her sides with his long, black claws and kissed her neck again. Her body awakened for a moment, but she shut it down. She knew nothing good could come of giving in to a demon.

Perhaps most of the world would think dreams were just dreams, but Farrah knew better. There were dreams, and then there was this—something dark and complex, and infinitely worse than any bad dream could be. Somehow this nightmare could leech into her reality. She'd started waking up with bruises from where she'd fallen in her dream. That very morning, she'd found scratches over her legs and arms from the heap of rocks she'd spent the night hiding in. Who knew what would happen to her if she gave him what he wanted?

Meanwhile, his touch grew bolder. He inflicted feather-light caresses upon her breasts while he licked up her neck to nibble her ear. She stared forward, her eyes wide open. If she closed them, she knew her body would take it as a sign of welcoming this pleasure. If she stared into the darkness that flickered with shapes and shadows, she could try to think of other things. Things that had nothing to do with the demon holding her.

He squeezed her breast, the tips of his claws digging in through her shirt, not tearing fabric or breaking skin, but just enough to indent her flesh and make her wince.

Submit.

She didn't bother with a reply. Over and over, she'd tried to communicate with the demon. He wouldn't converse, only say the same words, one at a time, more furiously the longer the night stretched. There was no reasoning with a monster.

A low growl vibrated through him, filled with impatience.

Tonight.

Her teeth gritted at the arrogance in his tone. His voice echoed with frustrating confidence in her mind.

Yet she felt it too. Something was different about tonight. How she didn't even recall falling asleep. How soon the darkness had come. How quickly he'd trapped her. She didn't understand how he'd caught her. Usually they were locked in an endless chase, but tonight he seemed to have more power over her dream.

The landscape blurred and changed. The hotel room returned, encased in near pitch-black darkness. The demon pushed her into the center of the room. Farrah looked around in desperation for an escape, but even though this was a replica of her hotel room, the doors were missing. The furniture was decaying as if centuries had passed. Light glowed along seams in the illusion, highlighting the corners of the room, the area beneath the couch where it sat on the floor, and the fractures along the walls—just enough illumination to show the demon's features as he stood before her.

His appearance was already burned into her

memory, but still gave her a moment of shock. Tall horns curved away from his forehead, adding to his already impressive height. He was bulky and muscular, and his skin was the mottled color of hot coals, sooty gray and black with faintly glowing veins of red as if lava flowed in his veins.

The crimson vessels stretched over his strong thighs and snaked around the thick column of his cock. She hated that she'd noticed, but there was no avoiding the sight of it. The first night she'd seen him, she'd known exactly what he wanted. A demon wouldn't have that for no reason.

Heat flooded her body and smoke filled her nostrils as her clothing singed away completely. Her hands flew to cover her sudden nakedness. She turned away and hesitated, again realizing there was nowhere to run.

Something wrapped around Farrah's left ankle, then her right. She glanced down to see the ground twisting and writhing to hold her captive. She yanked at her legs until her muscles hurt, but she couldn't break free. Struggling made her fall forward, and she landed hard on her hands and knees.

Lovely.

He was on her in the next instant, pressing his nude form against her back. He nestled his thick cock between her thighs, hot and throbbing, but didn't enter.

She clenched her eyes shut against the sensation

of him and everything it did to her body. Though she was as terrified as she always was, a part of her—a teeny, tiny sliver—responded with something other than fear.

He planted his hands on either side of her and shoved his hips forward, grinding his hard length along her folds. He slid against her again and again, rubbing the ridged texture of his cock against her pussy and igniting her sensitive clit. At first there was friction, but it didn't last. Soon her slick arousal spread over him, and he used it to slide up and down her channel, her pussy lips spreading easily.

Farrah's cheeks heated with embarrassment. This was better than fearing for her life, but it shocked her how easily her fear had allowed pleasure to sink in. She had to fight not to writhe against him, had to hold her breath not to moan. She liked it rough, and she'd been alone for far too long. Her body reacted based on memories and long-ignored cravings.

His cock wasn't smooth like a man's. It was rough. Coarse, raised bumps along his length tormented her, the sensation blurring her thoughts and rationale. His dominating and possessive nature called to something within her, a whisper of longing that welcomed his crudeness and the way he took what he wanted.

The demon curled his body over hers and dug one clawed hand into the dusty ground beside her shoulder to steady himself. Soot filled her nostrils and choked her, but the discomfort was negligible when compared to the churning sensations of wicked pleasure within her. He reached his other hand around to grasp her breast, massaging it eagerly. His claws dug at the full flesh of her breast in a way that excited her. The danger made her lightheaded, yet she felt oddly safe within the cage of his limbs.

Her eyes fluttered, the last remnants of her common sense screaming at her. What was she doing? Was she really going to give in now? The hand around her breast twisted her nipple until she gasped, and then it slid down her stomach and between her thighs. The demon spread his fingers on either side of her pussy, pressing the head of his cock against her entrance.

All logic fled her. She held her breath and waited.

He pushed in, and he was so large as to make Farrah squirm and grunt. After only a few seconds, it felt like too much, the pressure and stretch an aching burn even though she was wet and ready. She whimpered and cursed, but he continued to sink in without hesitation.

After a few more agonizing minutes, he withdrew an inch—she sucked in a breath—and then he shot his hips forward, thrusting back in deeper and rougher. Her breath shook free in a sharp cry and she sank to her elbows. Something seemed to trigger in the demon and he snarled at her back. He plunged in farther, and quicker, becoming more bestial and aggressive with each thrust.

She arched her back and her torso bowed, pressing her bare breasts to the ground. Though gritty, it was cool, and the chill contrasted perfectly with the heat of the demon's body curled over her and in her. Her breathing grew shallow. The pain had gone, now a distant soreness. Pleasure had replaced it, an alluring, demanding tide that bubbled deep within her. He felt like nothing she'd ever known or could imagine. He was harder than any man—thicker and hotter too. His cock grazed every inch of her inner walls, burnishing her with the rough mold of his shaft. She felt each of his raised ridges, and with each second, grew dizzier from the overwhelming sensation.

His hand returned to her breast just as he slammed so deep his sac collided with her sensitive mound. His previous thrusts had kissed and bruised her cervix, and this last blow was like a battering ram to her insides. Black spots danced across her already dark and blurry vision. Then he rammed in again, and the shock sent goosebumps over her entire body. Her nipples ached. Her toes curled. The beginning of tears caught on her lashes. She screamed in pain or pleasure; it was impossible to separate the two.

She didn't understand what was happening. She didn't understand why it felt so damn good. She was being forcefully fucked—no, *used*—by a demon, and she couldn't think straight.

"No more," she pleaded.

He grabbed her shoulder with one hand and snatched a tangle of hair in the other, curving her back further, forcing her into an uncomfortable, nearly painful position. Her breath came in gasps as he held her there, thrusting harder, the power behind each stroke shaking her body and making her breasts bounce as moans staggered from her throat. He pulled on her shoulder to aid in pushing deeper into her, as if he'd impale her—as if he couldn't get far enough inside her to fuck her properly. It hurt, but the ache thrilled her.

Pleasure built low in her belly, a confusing frenzy of sensations fed not only by his cock striking deep inside her, but by the way he tugged sharply on her hair and the danger and excitement of being ravaged by a monster. Her nerves drew taut, and she held her breath until the dam broke and she froze, unable to move while pleasure flooded her senses. Her muscles gave out, and she felt dizzy and limp as her body continued to sway and shake to his actions. Her orgasm shot through her in sporadic bursts, leaving parts of her numb and tingling and over-stimulated. For a moment her body seemed to accommodate him with ease, but as the euphoria of her climax faded, his bruising thrusts became agonizing to her lust-swollen folds.

"Too much," she whimpered, struggling in his hold.

He growled in response, or at least she thought it was a response, until he struck deep and held himself there. Her inner walls trembled, clenching and seeking relief, and then his cock spasmed and filled her with heat. She felt each powerful twitch of his shaft as it surged, sending his seed flooding into her depths. The strange sensation sent another fluttering orgasm through her, making her writhe. This made him grasp her tighter, his claws digging into her shoulder as he held her still and emptied his cock.

His entire body vibrated as he finished and stilled, and Farrah slumped forward as he released her. She collapsed, spread out on the cool ground, exhausted and dazed. The motion pulled him free of her, and then the fullness she'd become used to vanished, replaced by the wet sensation of cum dripping down her thighs.

She closed her eyes and tried to catch her breath, sucking in air as if she'd been saved from drowning. It was over. She would wake now, wouldn't she? But even then, she'd feel forever changed by the encounter. It felt like she'd surrendered something to him, something unspoken and complicated.

After wiping her face with shaking hands, she looked back across her sweat-dampened shoulder and saw him. He was sitting back on his haunches and staring at her. The darkness obscured his face so that she couldn't see his eyes, but it still felt as if she were being scrutinized.

The tightness around her ankles slipped away, and she rolled to her side. The urge to run returned, thrumming in her veins weakly, but consistently. A strange calm descended. The atmosphere changed. The shock and trembling in her body resolved, and she managed to sit up. She scooted away from him with every intent of escaping.

Farrah.

He'd never said her name before, and hearing it now made her breath catch. He reached one hand out. The darkness flickered, and for a moment, his claws vanished to reveal a very human hand, fingertips outstretched toward her. Yet within a blink, his claws returned. He sometimes distorted this way, and she was never sure if it was her imagination or not. It was a nightmare, after all. The concept of real versus imagined was stretched thin and folded over itself.

He cocked his head, long horns catching the flickers of light beyond him in a terrifying silhouette. She shivered, and once again, everything within her vision flashed with light to paint a different scene. For a moment his horns disappeared, and a piercing blue light shone from where his eyes would be, were he not cloaked in shadows.

He crawled toward her, and she watched, entranced. His appearance changed within blinks, back and forth like a strobe light between demon and something else. Something more human. Something vaguely familiar.

When he reached her, however, he was fully a demon again, and a deep growl shook from him. Her surroundings changed again as well, no longer a shadowed version of her hotel room, but the hellish landscape she'd seen before. She still rested against a surface, but it was now a bright mirror. She looked down and saw her own frightened expression staring back. Then she saw him looming over her. The mirror gave light to him, and now his eyes were visible—hard and glossy black. He gripped her left foot and yanked, sliding her back to him, so that she was between his squatting thighs.

Her gaze snared on the thick swell of his cock. She could see it fully now, and her first thought was to marvel at how he'd ever managed to shove it all inside her. Seeing it made her ache. Her pussy clenched at the memory of what they'd just done. It glistened with their mingled fluids, the very sight making her stomach quiver. She felt empty now, and hated how much she wanted to *not* be empty.

Looking up, she knew he'd caught her staring. A smile curved on his lips before he chuckled, baring gleaming, sharp teeth. The sight and sound unsettled her, and she yanked at her foot in his grasp.

Stay.

The command came with a jolt of force that

momentarily locked her muscles in place. That he could affect her that way scared her, but she didn't resist. She watched him as he rose, one hand on his cock. Eyes locked on her, he stroked its massive length, growing harder. One glance up at his face and she knew what he wanted. Whether it was a hidden mental command or her own depraved desires, she wasn't certain, but she rose to her knees.

She swallowed as she got a closer look at him, her hand lifting to touch him of its own accord. His shaft was wide and eager, the skin stretched over the straining muscle beneath. She gripped him with a surge of daring. The ridges along his cock throbbed and hardened against her palm. She dragged a fingertip over one and it reacted, transforming from a rigid bump to a nearly sharp barb. They'd felt amazing inside her, and she blushed as she admitted it to herself.

Then Farrah brought her second hand to him. If she wrapped them both around his shaft, her fingertips touched and overlapped to the first section of each joint. He was huge, and holding him like this made her body stir. She became warm, yet uneasy about how she could practically feel her body gushing with slick arousal. That part of her anticipated more. The desire to escape lingered, but it was not nearly so strong.

Sliding her grip up, she brushed the flared collar of his cock's head. It pulsed and swelled with desire.

The demon snarled, and the sound was clearly one of satisfaction, not displeasure. Moisture wept from the dark slit centered on his tip. She couldn't resist. She bent forward and probed the slit with her tongue, collecting the fluid there.

He was bitter and spicy, and somehow exactly how she'd imagined a demon might taste. It was strangely intoxicating in a way that made no sense, but Farrah didn't bother overthinking it. Instead she licked around the head of his cock, tasting the remnants of their sex. It was dirty and depraved, and it made her hunger for more.

The pull of her hair gave her pause as the demon reached into the dark curls and held them the way men liked to hold women during oral sex. The sort of grip that was half "let me hold your hair for you," and half "I'm going to hold your head while I fuck your mouth." In this case, however, the insistent scrape of his claws against her scalp let her know that if she wasn't careful, he'd likely fuck her throat with the same fervor he'd used to bruise her insides.

The imagined threat sent a renewed flow of excitement through her, threaded with fear. He likely saw her as holes to be used. It wouldn't be farfetched to assume he wouldn't let her go until she was sore everywhere. That realization didn't worry her, but it should have.

An impatient tug made her redirect her focus. She stroked up and down along his shaft, fascinated by the way it responded, its texture changing as his arousal grew. Pressure on her scalp forced his cock-head between her lips, and she sucked and licked to keep up with the slowly increasing tempo of his rocking hips. She barely had room to swallow, and soon her saliva dripped down his length, aiding her deliberate tugs on his cock.

He forced himself deeper and deeper, until Farrah planted one hand firmly on his length to keep him at bay. His frustration broke through with a growl that vibrated through his entire body and sent a chill down her spine. She closed her eyes as he plunged his cock deeper, breaking her grip on his shaft, until he hit the back of her throat, making her gag and flinch. He dug his claws into her scalp, scratching and twitching. He ignored her struggling and drove in and out of her mouth, fucking her throat and gaining no depth, but leaving her unable to breathe or even think. Tears burned in her eyes from the discomfort and the desperation to suck in air. She no longer gagged, but choked and suffocated. She dug her own nails into his thighs, but his skin was like leather. She couldn't scratch him. He gave no indication of acknowledging her struggle, except that she suspected it made his cock even harder and more unrelenting.

Her pulse thudded in her ears, deafening. The world swam out of focus, and she closed her eyes.

Farrah came to and coughed as the demon slid his dick free of her throat. It took her a moment to stop coughing, and then to realize that she'd lost consciousness. It was probably only for a few seconds, but long enough to douse her hot arousal in the chill of reality.

She clutched her throat and stared up at him. Darkness swathed his face, but she sensed smugness and pride pouring from him. She looked away and pinched her arms. It never worked to wake her, but she still tried. She wouldn't survive this much longer. She trembled from head to toe, lightheaded and exhausted. She needed to wake.

Farrah groaned as she tried to stand and crumpled back down to her knees. The demon laughed. The sound echoed in her head, taunting her.

So close. Submit.

She glared at him. "Fuck you."

No. I'll fuck you.

She froze at his reply, which was the closest they'd ever come to a conversation.

I'll fuck you until you submit. And then I'll fuck you harder. More. Forever.

Bracing herself against the threat, she forced herself to ask, "You can talk now?"

Now that I'm sated enough to think straight.

"And that means—"

Enough talk.

He stepped forward, his erection jutting out. It visibly throbbed, and she stared. The darkness flickered, and within it, the demon's moan slithered through her. When she could see again, she didn't understand what lay before her. His cock had doubled, not in size, but in number. Another appendage sat above the other, as if cloned.

Farrah's jaw dropped and her heart jumped in her chest, ready to beat through her ribcage with terror. She turned, but couldn't move an inch farther before he hauled her back against his body. She struggled, arms swinging and legs kicking with renewed vigor, but he wrestled her down. With one hand, he trapped her wrists high above her head, suspending her over his lap. Her bent legs rested on his muscular thighs. The head of one cock slid against her rear entrance.

"No, no, no," she pleaded, the words falling from her lips with shaky breaths. "Not two."

It has to be two.

"Why? Why is any of this—"

We both want to fuck you. We both need to breed you. The voice paused, and she could hear the smirk lacing his words. *We won't go there tonight. Tonight, we breed. That means...*

He trailed off, vanishing from her mind. Then he lowered her, and his cocks slid in the lingering wetness of her earlier arousal, but with no insistence.

He caressed the front of her body, tweaking her nipples and sighing in pleasure as he did so. Eventually, his touch made it between her thighs. He shoved two clawed fingers into her heat, making her flinch and freeze at the same time. Though they slipped into her easily, she held her breath in fear of the damage the sharp edges could cause. She felt only the slight thickness of them, however, working in and out. He separated his fingers within her, as if testing her or stretching her. She realized what he meant to do, but she couldn't think of it—she refused to. Any moment now, she'd wake up.

Her hips had their own motivation, though. They rocked and rode his fingers, and she bit her lower lip to keep from making a sound of anticipation. She bit until she bled.

Then his fingers were gone, and he reached between their bodies to grip both cocks. He brought them to her entrance and prodded. She almost wanted to laugh at the ridiculousness of it. It wouldn't work. He couldn't... She couldn't...

He pistoned upward, and the stinging sensation of being stretched wide had her gasping and cold. He released her arms and she fell farther onto his cocks, unsupported by his strength. She couldn't think through the pain, only cry out with each breath as she tried, but failed to lift her body from his. He held her hips and forced his way deeper, invading and crowding her pussy.

At first, everything was too tight. She could feel his struggle, and she gritted her teeth as he tried to move in and out, only to seem stuck. He curled over her writhing body and sank his teeth into the slope of her neck. The new sensation helped distract her. He grabbed her breast again and fondled it roughly. It took her a moment to realize he meant to give her some pleasure in the hopes that it would relax her. But there was no relaxing; her muscles had seized around him, yet still he sought to cram himself into her.

While he rolled her nipple between two fingers, he used his free hand to grasp one of hers. He led it between her thighs and forcefully rubbed her hand over her pussy. He couldn't rub her clit himself, she realized—not with those claws. She didn't want to aid him, yet she wanted the pain to subside.

Farrah closed her eyes and slid her fingertips up and down her folds to collect her slick arousal before drawing them to her clit. She bit her tongue and concentrated on that, and on his hands, both of which now massaged her breasts.

It occurred to her that if he were truly a monster, he wouldn't bother softening her up. Surely a demon cared nothing about tearing into her flesh to gain his pleasure. What did it mean that he'd rather coax her to relax?

The thought gave her pause, but only briefly, as his caresses sank through her defenses. The heat of their bodies flowed like a blanket over her, soothing her. Her inner walls relaxed as her pleasure grew, and he drove in deeper, but the pain was a distant ache now.

She leaned back against him as he flicked his tongue over her neck. His rumble was pleasant and satisfied, and she matched it with a soft moan.

Soon he was thrusting deep and hard, each cock pulsating within Farrah and jolting her senses. She felt full to bursting, and when the twin tips reached her end, her walls spasmed and sent an instant, overwhelming climax through her. She rode the waves of euphoria as he fucked her, his intensity increasing until she heard the wet sounds of flesh slapping flesh.

She came down from her bliss, only to be met with an insatiable desire for more. She placed her hands over his where he touched her breasts, and he understood her intention, removing his hands to allow her to touch herself. Instead he clutched her waist and pistoned himself up and up, until his every stroke slammed into the end of her channel.

The sensation was a chaotic blend that left Farrah lightheaded and delirious, as if she were stuck on a continuous orgasm. Her body cramped and convulsed against his plundering cocks, and she welcomed them still. As it went on, her head rolled back against him and she ceased to think or care about anything but the pleasure. She could feel him cresting too, feel the muscles of his arms tighten, his torso flexing against her back. She nearly begged for him to finish, not because she wanted it to end, but because she wanted to feel his climax. One of his hands came up and wrapped around her throat, not cutting off her air completely, but enough that the tension heightened her pleasure.

Holding her there, he froze at the height of a devastating thrust. His cocks pulsed and throbbed, and he groaned above her ear. His chest heaved as he panted. Farrah had no energy to react except to lean harder against him, barely able to keep herself upright.

Then he relaxed his grip, and they sat together in silence as the world continued to flicker with distant lights and moving shadows. He lifted her from his lap and lay her on the ground on her back. Farrah simply breathed and kept her eyes closed, recovering, as she heard and felt him moving around her. She didn't stir until he lifted her again.

Smooth skin rubbed against hers, startling her. Stranger still was the way he touched her with care and gentleness. She was cradled against a pale, warm chest, and she was almost afraid to look up and see the demon's new face. She had a suspicion. Her breathing quickened, and the scent of peppery cologne lingered in the air—a scent she knew too well.

With his thumb, he stroked her cheek. "I'm so sorry," he murmured. "I could barely..."

The voice struck her. She dared herself to look up, and there he was, no longer the demon, but her lover. The shock of seeing him now left her speechless for a moment. Her thoughts conflicted, and she had trouble pulling anything together over the steady flow of heat and pleasure from his touch. It was like rising above quicksand, but she eventually did it.

"Nathan," she rasped.

He nodded.

Tears filled her vision, blurring her vision of him —her fiancé, Nathan, killed a year ago this month, just weeks before their wedding.

"Is this a trick?" She shook her head. "Please don't play games with me."

"No game." He bent down and kissed her. His kiss was gentle and familiar, and heartbreaking. Their tongues entwined, and he tasted like he always had, sweet and masculine. It was as if no time had passed. As if he'd never died and left her.

"How?" she asked when he pulled away. She cupped his smooth, warm jaw, a part of her not believing that what she touched was real.

"You wished for me. Over and over." He looked around them where the hellscape continued to flicker. "It reached me when your grief was winning out."

"I don't understand."

"I don't entirely understand it myself. But he does—the other part of me. The part I found while trapped here. Something about you, about us, has opened some sort of way out for me."

She studied his face. He looked exactly like he had the last time she'd seen him. His blue eyes sparkled, even in the darkness. His black hair fell over his forehead in its usual carefree manner. She kept waiting for the darkness to move over him and change him.

"You're not making any sense," she said. "Not that any of this makes any sense."

"I love you."

"I love you too," she whispered, her voice failing her.

"Can you forgive me? For what we—for what I did?"

The joy of holding him, kissing him, of seeing him up close after all this time, made Farrah momentarily forget the rest of the night. The nightmares and the chasing. The pain and the rough coupling. The unexplainable yearning in her response, and the way that somehow, even though it made no sense, she had felt cherished.

"You're the demon," Farrah said.

"He's a part of me, born of what it took to survive the torment here." His expression grew distant, and a chill invaded his voice. "Though survival is relative. You're dreaming, so you don't see everything that I see. Everything that's here, ready to rip and tear and destroy."

"I don't understand," she confessed. "I know I said that, but this is too much."

He shook his head and softened his tone. "I can explain it all with time. But you have to decide right now, before it's too late. When you wake, I can be with you." He kissed her forehead. "I can return to you."

"What?" Her mind raced, disbelief swept beneath a torrent of joy.

"During the day, I'll be Nathan. But each night, the demon has to return." He looked down at her naked body, but instead of heat in his gaze, there was conflict. "And he'll want you. Sharing your body with him is all I can do to tame him."

"But it's you," she whispered.

"Yes." His face twisted with regret. "I don't want to hurt you, he just... We know your limitations. It's still a dream..."

She stroked her thumb across his cheek, memories assailing her. Her love for him hadn't changed. Her desire to have him hadn't waned. Damn it, she'd missed him. Now she was holding him, and she had a chance to keep him.

"It's real, though," she told him. "Something about these dreams follows me back."

"This world is real, but we can't do actual damage to you." Nathan frowned and exhaled, nuzzling her open palm. "We're connected now. We share the pain and the pleasure, and I want to tell you more, but I'm afraid you'll wake up soon..."

At last, she could have him back with her; that was all she heard. That was all that mattered.

"Yes!" she exclaimed. "Yes!"

Nathan searched her face before giving a slight nod. "Then lie back, love. I'm not done with you. Neither is he. We'll make the most of this dream, and when you wake, we'll make the most of our future."

MORE FROM GODIVA

We hope you enjoyed ***Demon of Her Dreams*** by Godiva Glenn!

Find more wild romance in the *Night Wolves* series.

How can Charlotte walk away when she's finally found where she belongs?

Charlotte shook off the shackles of the human world and is struggling to find her place amongst the Lupine. Within the Bronze pack, everyone has a path and she's eager to find hers. Yet thoughts of romance begin to cloud her mind as she finds herself surrounded by blissfully mated couples.

Godiva Glenn is a nocturnal being, much like vampires and cats. She holds a B.A. in Literature, which more or less means she has spent more hours reading and writing than she would ever care to admit to. Luckily, all that knowledge comes in handy for her creative pursuits.

Most of her recent writing endeavors circle around the paranormal/supernatural. Wolves are her preferred sexy shifters, but who knows what the future holds.

She resides in the U.S. with dreams of traveling abroad to research locations.

WWW.GODIVAGLENN.COM

INVADED

BY CASS ALEX

INVADED

CASS ALEX

DAYZEE

I MADE IT HERE ALIVE! Today marked day 1 at UGP outpost 7*KUr.

Why the Unified Governing Patrol felt they needed me on *this* particular planet, I have no idea. It's hot, it's humid, I've never met any of the species living nearby, and it turns out they all barely tolerate each other and probably hate us. Lucky me! It looks like I'll be assigned here for the next half a year, minimum. I'd say I'm gonna need more chocolate but it would never survive this heat.

I did get to walk the perimeter of the camp when I arrived, while my new commander briefed me on my assignment. CDR Firken was cute! Single, early 30's, and I think he's a Pisces.

The base has two neighboring species that

appear to heavily dislike each other and the UGP seemed to think that a sociologist with psych training could possibly make a difference. Let's be real — they just didn't have a Species Specialist available so they had to settle for me. I'll take what I can get and try to make a name for myself.

The nearby aggression appears to be a dispute over a shared section of land. That area has some type of fruit-bearing trees, possibly with rooted vegetables and herbs nearby, and both species use them for sustenance.

I need to study the two separate groups and the shared land in question and report back my findings. The goal will be to figure out what needs to be done to find peace between them since their upset is riling up all the *other* species out here.

I've seen — albeit low-quality — pictures of these things and I'm thinking the last thing they want to do is hold hands and sing Kumbaya. Hell, one doesn't even have hands, just layers of tentacles.

I need to find a way to communicate with them without them feeling invaded by us newcomers.

Aside from that, the sleeping quarters here are small bungalow-style houses just big enough for a bed, a footlocker, a small table and chairs, a toilet and sink behind a divider, and the world's smallest kitchenette.

I'll call it cozy and leave it at that. At least I am

not in the barracks and for that I am grateful. Well, except for shower time.

DAYZEE

Well, it's day three and I finally got to see the neighbors. They're interesting, to say the least.

One is a bird-like hybrid species that nests in the local cave system, located just above a large section of the beach. The rocky alcove slopes down to the sand and is riddled with large holes that the species has taken over as its nests.

They have colorful 'feathers' around the crown of their head and down their backs which look to be stiff and sharp, and a fan-like 'tail' that they can open and brandish. I saw this happen with one particular bird-man when he spotted a squid-guy nearby — he rattled his ass feathers at him in warning.

The rest of their bodies look soft and downy. They have shorter arms with quad-digited 'hands' tipped in claws, and their downy legs look powerful and end in large-boned feet with sharp talons. If a T-Rex and a bird screwed a human, this might be their kid. They also have large almond-shaped eyes, and their 'beaks' are more like humanoid noses but slightly hooked in appearance. They all have different facial expressions and personalities, but the one I am studying, his default setting appears to be 'cranky'.

The other species is some sort of cephalopod hybrid. A squid-octopus type being that stands upright and actually has an elegant gait despite having many limbs. I wasn't positive these were even sentient until I saw one interact with one of the bird guys. They kept their distance but appeared to yell and threaten each other. I may have my work cut out for me.

The octo-squid has eight arms plus the two extra-long snake-like tentacles but they radiate from the body like they would an octopus, and are thicker and stronger like an octopus. There are two layers with the upper being slightly thinner than the lower, and I thought I saw smaller tentacles between the layers. Their head shape is somewhat bulbous and extends into a mild crown, and they have multiple eyes. None that I saw have less than two, or more than nine. They have a flatter, sloped nose, a mouth, and many facial expressions. They seem easy-going and social.

Next goal: Seem harmless enough that they won't attack when they meet me, yet friendly enough that they engage with me.

I'm not a miracle worker, people! Remember that when it's time for a raise review. Maybe if I do well enough I can switch to that nice little bungalow at the corner of the territory. It has its own shower!

Oh, and CDR Firken smiles and nods when he goes by but hasn't talked to me again. The others just pretend I am invisible. Literally invisible. Some asshole stepped on me as I tried to walk past him. I know I'm short but give me a break, I know he saw me.

If this keeps up I am going to make sock puppets and talk to myself because it's going to be a really lonely six months.

KHAW

I arose from my nesting spot and moved to the opening of the cover to feel the heat of the rising glows on my quillens. My face raised to the skies, my eyes closed as I spared a moment to enjoy my awakening. The air was ripe with the scent of bloomings and nectar pods from the nearby eating sources, and the sounds of many creatures beginning their globe durations.

No sooner had I slid back both of my lids when suddenly there he was. That zotlsh from the wet. My eyes narrowed on him as I watched him rise from the wet and move slowly towards the feeding sources. He tended towards the ground ones as much as the nectar pods, but I did not like to share either with him. There was something about this one of the wet that I simply Did. Not. Like.

I stomped my lower talons at him and loudly shook my quillens. My warning growls barked in low huffs from me in an attempt to ward him away from the feeding sources. And also from the new creatures that have settled nearby as they had no talons or fangs, and seemed defenseless as they roamed nearby areas in their flesh coverings.

Hearing my warnings, he paused and glanced at me, several of his eyes narrowing when his gaze caught mine. Immediately his many long flesh talons rose into the air waving at me. I think he may have even inflated himself to appear more threatening when he hissed his language at me. How dare he! I responded by rattling louder and threatening to raise my crown quillens. My barked huffs were shorter and more aggressive, letting him know his presence offended me.

His flesh talons picked up debris from the ground, throwing them in my direction. I was too far away for them to touch me but I recognized his combative behavior. If he wanted aggression, I would bring him aggression!

I started down the ledge towards the feeding grounds.

GLUUB

I arose from the water, my limbs raising me up once the delicate waves delivered me to the surface and deposited me on the grains. Suddenly basking in the bright warmth, I took a moment to greet the day. Yet again I lived to see a turn of the brightness, and for this I was grateful.

The rumbling of my innards disturbed my peace and I glanced towards the land-food source area. I was aware new beings had come, and we were told to avoid them, but my nature was curious and I hoped to see one. Usually, all I saw were the noisies.

The noisies lived in the hole in the rocks just above the sand. There was a group of them but one in particular made aggressive noises — sharp guttural barks and threats — and we grew tired of them long enough that we tended to keep our distance. It was simply not our way.

But today? Today I see one of them making hate eyes at me and shaking himself. This one I have seen before many times. Often we rise at the same period and my existence he instantly takes offense to. Most awakenings I try to ignore him because I do not like his noise and threats, and he never brings me any peace.

He seems like he might also be making noises at me again this day but luckily I am too far to have to deal with him. Once again I stand tall and wave my limbs at him in greeting. I try each day. He responds harshly, as usual, so today I mock his threatening movements.

There was one in every group. And in that group, he was that one.

I shook off my angst and moved towards the land-food source. I heard more aggressive rattling and I stopped to eye him. "What now?" I yelled, asking him.

He slammed his limbs to the ground in jerky movements and waved his color blades at me. It was to be one of *those* awakenings, it seemed. Already this being made me feel tired.

I puffed up to my full height, picking up stone rounds and wood brokens and waving them before half-heartedly throwing them in his direction. How did he like it? What a glurk!

He rattled louder and I turned and completely ignored him, choosing instead to seek out food. Maybe I would finally get to see one of the new beings.

DAYZEE

Guess what I got to see today — the Aviarids and the Octocephs interacting!

I had to name them in order to send info to the

UGF, so here we are. But as I was saying, they interacted and I watched. However, I don't know what I witnessed.

When I snuck into the area they forage in, I came across two of them attempting to communicate. They were at the beach still so I watched from behind the trees, hidden amongst the foliage and some kind of bramble.

I think the Aviarid had a temper tantrum, but I am not quite sure. Maybe it was a seizure? There was some odd barking, and he rattled his 'feathers' while stomping the ground. And the Octoceph waggled his tentacles at him. I couldn't tell if it was friendly or not. Only half his six eyes were on the Aviarid though, the rest were eyeing the trees.

Then they both suddenly stopped and went to grab food while still warily watching each other.

I think they knew someone else was there, even though I stayed hidden. They purposely chose the tree I was behind, instead of any of the others, and were slow as they chose their fruit. Cautious, even.

They seemed big from afar but were even larger up close. At 5'4", I felt like I was standing near football players. They were at least a foot taller than me and twice as wide. It's harder to tell with the Octoceph, but man that Aviarid is buff! He those shoulders he would have to angle to fit through a doorway.

The Octoceph was the first to depart and before he did one of his pieces of fruit rolled down a tentacle and into the dense bramble I was peeking out from, landing just a few feet from me. I nearly panicked. The Aviarid huffed, staring between the fruit and the Octoceph like he was offended. When the Octoceph walked away, the Aviarid seemed confused, staring between the tree and the spot where the fruit rolled to, like he was expecting something. He left a minute or two later, seeming reluctant. They didn't fight after that though, they just went back to their sides of the beach.

When it was safe I came out from behind my tree and picked up the fruit and brought it back with me. The physicians here all swear that it is safe for me to eat and that we don't have them regularly only because there are no fruit trees on our section of land. I don't know what this fruit is called but it is the size of a grapefruit, has a thicker outer skin like an apple, and the inside taste and consistency reminds me of a very sweet peach. It had five small round seeds inside so I stole a bowl from the canteen and dirt from near the fruit trees, and I planted the seeds. That area seemed lusher than ours so I am hoping the soil is nice and fertile. It's in the window of my little sleeping quarters soaking up rays.

GLUUB

The past few turns, something has changed with the very aggressive noisy. Instead of making hate eyes and sharp sounds and shaking his color blades, he simply stands and watches me.

Today I stood still and returned his gaze. I have not waved my limbs at him in greeting either, as last time he chose to come to me at the land-food source and nearly feared the newcomer hiding behind the foods.

I could scent them there and they smelled pleasant. I considered that they were also there to eat and I wondered if they ate the globe food I gifted to them. Maybe next time they will greet me.

The noisy could have easily caused the new one to run away from all his sounds but once I rolled the globe the noisy became completely quiet for the first time. Did he also sense the newcomer? Did he make noise at them once I returned to the water?

I carefully waggled two limbs at him, once up and once down. He tilted his head to consider me, as if I was something to figure out, but did not make threats this time.

We remained watching each other without a sound. We stared at each other until he shook his feathers lightly at me, only once, and then turned and retreated into his hole.

KHAW

This day when I rise, I remain in my nesting spot instead of meeting the rising glows. My thoughts have overtaken me completely and I need time to consider things.

It has been many nestings now since something altered. It began with the first day the new being was in the feeding grounds, hidden behind the eating source. She remained quiet and hidden and did not interact, but I could scent her. Definitely an egg-giver. I wonder if she has a mate?

When the one from the wet gave her food, I did not expect this gesture from him. I thought he might attack the new creature since he and me wish to battle but that did not occur. He even left us both in peace.

Past this, we have watched each other but did not try to battle again. When he moved his flesh talons at me it was not in threat, it seemed like greeting. When my tribes own egg-givers came down to the wet, he brought nestlings to greet them, and brought eats from the wet. This brought the egg-givers much happiness, both the wet-food, and seeing the hatchlings from those that live in the wet.

We also did not know they were able to gather food from the wet so easily! It often takes us a full duration of the glow and we only manage to capture a few.

It was a kindness and we did not know the ones from the wet were capable of this. Before I left to my nest, I greeted him with my quillens out of respect.

But it was the many glows that followed that I was now thinking on.

We still rose and saw each other first each day, but now we simply meet on the grains and go to eat together. And we met our new one from behind the tree! We introduced ourselves. Her name is D'zee, and the one from the wet in named G'lb, and I told them I am called K'aw. We started to learn to communicate with our faces and limbs, and we began to learn small words of each other. I also learned that G'lb and his kind only take from the top of the nectar pods, and they leave the lower for my tribe because their flesh talons are longer. Yet another kindness. They share and we did not know. What else are we mistaken of?

D'zee is one of the fleshy beings and she smells very good to me. G'lb and me both noticed that she does not scent of another. I began the opening of a mating dance for her, so she knows I have no egg sitter. She bared her mouth sharps at me and slammed her hands together. I could not tell if she wanted to battle and if I was engaging her, so I stopped until I understand what had happened.

I do not think she wishes to battle though,

because we three now meet each glow from up until down. I have learned that she bares her mouth sharps when she has joy. When she does it while huffing it means extra joy. She calls this feeling 'happy'.

I do not think we have seen her battle face or movements yet, and this is good as it means she welcomes my presence. And also G'lb's.

More confusing is that my time with them both is what I rise for now.

When S'qak called my tribe to remind us to be careful of the newest hatchlings, it upset me being away from D'zee and G'lb. My upset was noted but S'qak did not anger at me, he just asked if I found an egg giver. I... did not have a response. But I now look at my nesting spot and I wonder if I should invite them to stay. Would my tribe accept them? My instincts say to invite D'zee, but G'lb should come also. It is nice when it is three. When not, it feels like something is missing.

Recently D'zee gave us a gift that made me wish to dance for her again. D'zee brought hatchlings of the nectar pods! We watched as she put them into the grounding. She aided all of our futures by feeding us and our tribes. This made me feel things I have never felt before. Not even when she showed us that the angry greenery near the nectar pods are called 'brambles' and they make what she calls 'berries' which we can eat and taste good. Or that others of the grounding greens are edible as well. We had more food than we knew of. She is taking more away to make hatchlings from them as well.

Maybe she is planning for her own hatchlings when she becomes an egg-giver, so she can feed them. Will they be with me? With G'lb? Is she an egg-giver for someone else? I hoped not but I have seen another fleshy one walk with her sometimes by where she nests.

Recently G'lb and me went in the glow-down to try and see her in her nest. She was on the outside talking with a male fleshy and making 'happy' bared mouth sharps so we did not intrude. We did not like seeing her with the male fleshy... It upset both of our instincts.

During our retreat, we heard sounds and saw other fleshies in their nests. We think they were making hatchlings. They are very unlike us so we stayed and watched the process.

We got to see the fleshies without their coverings. They come in many different colors, both the flesh and the covers! The creatures mated in numerous positions. The females had a pouch or opening underneath them. The males elongated and entered into the pouch and moved a lot before depositing. In some of the nests the male restrained the female during mating. In some, the female restrained her male. In some they took turns cleaning each others parts using their mouth before they mated, and both seemed to enjoy that.

The one which fascinated me most was the one with three mating instead of two. Half of G'lb's eyes were on me and half on the matings as we watched. It is clear to us that we both want D'zee.

I know that I can protrude but I do not know if G'lb can. How do his people mate? In my tribe we enter our mate and spray our release, and did not move around. There is no joy, just making hatchlings. We do not respond as the fleshies do during mating, but the more we watched, the more I wanted to try this. I think G'lb did too. It seemed enjoyable. I very much wanted to try the mating of mouths that I saw. The one with that will use her mouth limb, not her sharps. And the one where you groom your partner with your mouth.

We presume that D'zee must look similar to the other fleshies we are seeing but can we both mate with her?

I can perform a mating dance again and see if she accepts me as hers. G'lb has not danced yet though. Why does he wait? Maybe it is that he does not have attractive quillens to wave, like I do. He is embarrassed. This is why he does not dance for her.

I can fix this!

DAYZEE

I can't believe I've been here like three months. If it wasn't for the calendar reminding me, I wouldn't even notice it. My days are filled with Khaw and Gluub and I'm not even close to mad about it.

Things have changed so much over the past couple of months. We are learning each other's languages and responses, and becoming more understanding of our differences. If you look at them now, you'd think they were brothers with a different mother. From morning until night, if you see one of us, you see all three, and you know what? It's actually nice.

Every time Khaw realizes he likes me (LIKES likes me, not regular likes me) he started showing off his 'quillens' and prancing around a bit. He struts, fans his tail feathers, fluffs himself up a bit, and makes his crown feathers bob up and down. I can't even make this up — I think it's a mating dance of some sort? If he can do that around a pole I could finally afford to finish my doctorate. Just kidding. Well, sort of.

A few days ago when he started his latest dance, he handed Gluub something. Feathers? I don't know where he got them from or what the purpose was, but he looked very expectant. I think he wanted Gluub to join in? Gluub and I both looked confused at the colorful gift. But it was... thoughtful. He got

Gluub to grip a few feathers and flail them about. Gluub did it, and it made Khaw really happy. Like REALLY happy. I think he actually chirp-tweeted a few notes of happiness, it was precious!

Gluub waved feathers, Khaw danced like his life depended on it, and I laughed and clapped and cheered. At the end, Khaw looked like he was king of the world and was so happy that he preened and tried to groom us. Well, he played with my hair and fluffed it, and kind of petted on Gluub, who looked mildly scandalized but quickly recovered. Then Khaw stood up as tall as he could and strutted around looking positively triumphant, flashing his tail feathers and crowing to the sky. I think he was singing. He looked so damn happy. Gluub and I shared looks over it and enjoyed seeing Khaw in such good spirits.

I may need to be more careful of my feelings. I find myself looking at them less and less like my work, and more like... friends. Maybe even more than friends.

Friends wouldn't notice that Gluub had really nice lips, or that his eyes were all shades of blues, or that Khaw nearly smiled in all his happiness. Friends definitely would not want to touch them, even casually.

The more I tighten my boundaries, the harder it is to maintain them.

I got permission yesterday from Captain Underpants (ie. CDR Firken) to bring them onto the base and over to see my room soon. Firken shall forever wear that nickname ever since he started trying to talk to me after hours wearing nothing but his skivvies. He was normal until I started spending all my time with Khaw and Gluub but apparently, he is one of *those* guys and only wants what someone else has.

Not that I belong to anyone else. Do I? Do they? Would that even work physically? Not that I can wonder that out loud. Or can even ask anyone. Do they even have genitals? I'm pretty sure Khaw is male but I have no idea what Gluub is. How do they even mate?

I have questions. I'm just not sure I am ready for the answers yet.

Plus this is my job, helping understand the natives and bring about peace. But the more I remind myself that this is 'just my job', the harder it is for me to accept that.

GLUUB

This day, Khaaww showed us how his kind play. He brought wood pieces interlaced into a curved form. He rested it on the ground and slapped it with what Daashee calls his 'feet' and it rolled and he chased after it. Daashee's beings do this also and call it 'fuut-boll' and she joined him to play. I pushed it with my lowest limbs and followed it's path also but I am slower on the grains instead of the waves. They played slower so I could join as well.

After, I brought my kind to meet them. An elder and some younglings, and we showed them how we play by following each other quickly in the waves then darting away before touching. Daashee called it 'taagg' and tried with Khaaww on the grains. He looked confused at first but was quick to learn. I am too slow on the grains but when we play in the water I will excel.

Then Daashee showed us a small game of her kind. She used shells and stone rounds. She made two lines in two directions, leaving nine openings, and the goal was to make three stones or three shells in a line while taking turns. She called it 'tiik taak too'. Only two can play this game and we took turns. Later, Khaaww and I played until the bright became dark and we could not see. It is a skill game. We liked this and wish more of this type of game.

Before Daashee went to her 'home', she wrapped her limbs around Khaaww. We have seen her kind do this in greet before but she did not wrap us before this. When she wrapped Khaaww she spoke, "Yuu arr sofftt. I thhott yuurr fehhrrs wuudd cuut mee". His claws touched at her backside. He breathed into her head strands and he looked at peace. Like when he hopped with his color blades and I waved his other blades. He was calm.

She seemed unsure to wrap me and then made a surprised sound and said, "Yuu donnt feel sliimee orr smell fissee." and wrapped me more. I wrapped her with many limbs and she made a content noise and showed her teeth. She calls this a 'smile'. She scented very nicely and I did not wish to unwrap from her.

Khaaww watched us and was not upset or behaving harsh at all. He seemed even calmer. Then I realized — he has not been aggressive in a very long time.

Once she returned to her kind, Khaaww pointed his claw to where she left, then to him and me, and I agreed.

Ours.

DAYZEE

I like them. Crap! I'm going to ruin my career or cause an interstellar incident, I just know it.

Khaw is more brawn than brain but he has calmed considerably since we first met, and accepts Gluub and I as if we were his own and you can tell. He sits closer to me, as if he is desperate to touch me but scared to make any sudden moves. He also wants us both around him or he becomes distraught and chews at his feathers. For someone that wants to act like a tough guy, he really is a big softy. A softy with golden kaleidoscope eyes that looks at me and Gluub like we are all that exists in the world. A softy that seems desperate for affection.

I am no longer convinced this is a trio of friends, not gonna lie.

Gluub is the more emotionally intelligent and self-aware one but isn't as obvious about his affections as Khaw is. However, when I hugged him for the first time he wasn't eager to let me go. In fact he buried his face to my shoulder and breathed me in. For a moment I felt like I was his lifeline. Like something changed with us at that moment. It isn't even safe for me to admit that I want to feel his lips on my neck the next time he buries his face there. He has the most perfect lips. Not to mention six beautiful blue eyes that scream of intelligence.

It didn't hurt that neither of them felt or smelled like what I thought they would. I used that to keep my distance but now I am out of self-imposed road blocks.

Khaw's back feathers are sharp so when he sits close to me he turns them away to protect me. The rest of him is soft and downy and when I hugged him I just wanted to snuggle into his down and stay there a while. His arms are shorter than average but he is big enough that he was still able to enfold me in them.

Gluub... is Gluub. He surprised me when he returned my hug. He surprised me even more when he was reluctant to let me go. And when he buried his face to my shoulder I got scared until I realized he was actually nuzzling me. It was super sweet. Somehow I thought he would be gross or cold, but he was none of that, not at all. His skin feels like my own and he is warm, and both of them have a lightly spiced natural scent that is appealing to me. A little too much so. And I don't think I am the only one because I thought I saw some bulging lower on Khaw's torso. PLEASE let that be a penis of some type!

And now I am left thinking things I shouldn't.

I am going to test our longterm possibilities and introduce some of my food to them tomorrow. Fingers crossed!

GLUUB

Today Daashee brought us what she calls a 'picnic'. It is a cloth you sit on and many containers of 'food'.

Khaaww and I did not realize that her food would be this different from ours. Different from both our land and our waves. Many differences. She fed us with her hands and we tasted all she shared. Some we need to adapt to, but many were pleasing. Khaaww ate much and had big eyes at the tastes. Daashee's kind makes much of their eats by 'cooking'. She will need to 'cook' food I bring from the waves, she said to us, but she will try them.

After the picnic we just rested and were quiet together. We are content just to be near each other and inside our own thinkings. Some of the times Daashee brings a 'book' and will look at it and turn the insides. Some of the times she talks loud from it in her language and we listen and learn.

When Daashee's face glows and she shows her teeth, she calls this 'happy' and 'smiling' and sometimes 'laugh'. Daashee makes me 'happy'.

Daashee and Khaaww... make me happy.

KHAW

This glow we visit D'zee's nest. We arrive when the glows are down so that less fleshies see us. First, we see her nesting hole. It is large. Her nesting spot is very soft and G'lb and me like it much. We rested on it and she said she needed a bigger one, but this is a good nest she made!

I wished to ask D'zee also about fleshy matings, so we showed her the other nest with three in it. We could view it from inside her nest. It was very close and the other see-hole looked towards D'zee's. They had false glow in their nest so we made her false glow sleep and we watched them and they could not see us.

They did not see us watching. Or learning.

Or trying.

DAYZEE

Well, apparently we are all voyeurs. I should be ashamed but the more I think on it, the more turned on I get.

During their visit last night, we turned off the light and watched Maria make out with Thomas and Greg through the window.

Shame on us! Kind of.

We watched the three of them go through all the motions of foreplay from Thomas pinning her hands and Greg kissing down her body, to kissing and oral sex, to the eventual fucking, where they took turns, changed positions a few times, and at some point Thomas sprayed her with his release before they finally collapsed.

By the time the three of them finished we stood in the darkness wrapped in our own thoughts, and the intensity in the room was so thick you could have cut it with a knife.

Gluub remained staring into their dark room, visibly thinking, while Khaw looked at me with such longing that I blushed.

After a couple minutes, Gluub got the reluctant Khaw to leave with him. I changed into my nightgown and laid down, thinking. Thinking led to thoughts of what we watched, and the intensity in the room during it, and my fingers made their way to between my legs to rub away my need. But it just wasn't working. I tried for several minutes but only managed to make myself more sexually frustrated. Ugh!

I was nearly asleep when I heard sounds outside.

Why do these doors not have peep holes? If it was Captain Underpants trying to get in, I was going straight to his commanding officer!

But it wasn't. I cracked the door open and a tentacle wrapped the edge of it, several blue eyes suddenly coming into view mere inches from my face.

"Gluub? Is everything okay?" I stepped to the side, opening the door for him. He slipped into the room and before I could close the door, feathers shoved in close behind him.

"Khaw, you too? What's going on?"

He responded by inhaling deeply. Both of their nostrils flared as their gazes zero'd in on me.

"D'zee..." Khaws gaze became sultry and I felt surprise ping through my system. "We can scent you." Oops.

Gluub floated closer to me, his limbs seeming to swirl in elegant patterns. His focus was intent and solely on me and I wondered for a moment if these tentacle swirls were his version of Khaw's feather-flaunting mating dance.

"Daashee we wished to share the remains of the turn with you. Yes?"

They waited for my response. Here is where the line was drawn. I had no clear idea of what they wanted or were thinking. What did *I* want?

"Are you asking to stay here and talk more?" I needed some clarification.

"D'zee we wish to share with you." Khaw moved closer, his golden eyes sparking as he stared his intent.

"Oh, sure, what did you want to share?"

"You." Glubs limbs encompassed me from

behind, reaching out to pull Khaw into a triple hug. I found myself sandwiched between them, both of their bodies pressing into mine, and heat pulsed through to my core.

I wanted this, and I couldnt pretend anymore. I'd spent all day every day with them for months now, and returning home by myself felt lonely and wrong. Why couldn't we spend the nights with each other as well? Gluub wasn't reliant on his ocean to sleep, Khaw could nest anywhere, and the UGP didn't care what I did on my own time, so what was stopping us?

I reached back over my shoulder and softly stroked a hand down Gluub's face. He tilted his face into my hand, encouraging me to touch him more. Oh, I intended to.

In front of me Khaw leaned in to nuzzle his face against mine. His claws combed lightly through my hair as a low hum began inside his chest.

As his eyes wandered over me, I liberated one strap from my nightgown, freeing an arm. His eyes caught the added skin and stayed there, staring. Then I freed my other arm, allowing my nightgown to fall from my body and pool at my feet.

I could hear the intake of air from both of them and knew their eyes were exploring my skin. I didn't have to see their faces to know they were appreciating the view and that made me feel like a queen.

Taking a chance, I reached out and tugged a tentacle around me, letting Gluub experience the feel of me. I took Khaw's hand as well, resting it on my shoulder. I could feel him exploring our differences under his hand. I returned the favor by reaching out to stroke my fingers over his down. So soft. He burbled out a muted sound in response and his head feathers quivered.

I ran my hand sideways across his massive chest before working my way down towards his stomach. An area began to bulge at his lower abdomen and I eyed it curiously.

"Khaw, what is that?" I tapped a fingertip lightly at the swell, which caused it to part down the center and a protrusion to burst forth from the opening, lengthening before my eyes.

Okay there was no mistaking what *that* was.

And also, HECK YES! I mentally fist-pumped.

I saw Gluub's face peer over my shoulder and all three of us stared down at Khal's member. He was pink and nearly as thick as my wrist, with no natural 'crown' at his mildly tapered tip. He was also still extending.

Oh, this was going to be fun.

I slowly reached my fingers out towards Khaw's member, watching Khaw for any sign that he did not want me touching him. When he moved his hips to purposely bump into my hand, I realized he wasn't about to decline my touch.

His length looked like someone took excess skin and wrapped it around and around until the steel bar beneath it was covered. The flesh itself had the feel of a corkscrew twist, and I couldn't help but wonder what he would feel like inside of me. At his base was a small empty pouch.

I recalled learning that a male erection grows into any loose skin, and wondered if that meant he might get even bigger.

Before I got to touch him I let out a squeak as tentacles suddenly lifted me into the air and Gluub deposited me on my bed. He was at the foot of it and Khaw moved to my side. Almost immediately his top tentacles reached and drew my arms up above me, securing them there while his lower ones gripped my ankles and spreading my legs. His two longer, thinner limbs roamed over my skin as if examining me. I shivered as they stalked over me, my skin already feeling oversensitive. He wrapped a limb around a breast and squeezed it lightly. When my nipples hardened in arousal, he used the flat tips of his thinner, whiplike tentacles to encircle them. Once secured, he tugged, eliciting a moan from me that I did not realize existed. That caught Khaw's attention fast and he leaned over to run a raspy tongue over an entrapped tip. I think I may have squirted a little bit with that. It was looking like they both learned a lot from watching the neighbors earlier.

Gluub brought a tentacle tip to my lower slit, drawing it through and removing it coated lightly in my wetness. He brought it up to his face, smelling it before letting the tip disappear into his mouth.

"Mmmm..."

Khaw's attention snapped to him and I watched as Gluub drew the same tentacle through my wetness again, this time offering it to Khaw. No time was wasted and the tip of a limb disappeared into Khaws mouth. He sucked, his eyes dilating before the tentacle retreated. In a heartbeat he went from standing next to my side, to leaning over me and burying his face at my heat. I felt his tongue penetrate me, going right to the source of my honey as he began to lick me both inside and out.

Good heavens, I wasn't convinced I would survive this.

I also recognized this as something we watched earlier and remembered what Maria did during it. I tilted to the side and ran my tongue over his extended member. With no crown I was unsure where the most sensitive spot would be so I licked him from base to tip then swirled my tongue along his top, and watched for reactions.

I hadn't needed to worry — the second my tongue touched him he froze mid-lick and became so ramrod stiff he defied gravity. So I did what any good partner would do to someone just learning... I threw him into the deep-end. I opened my mouth and engulfed him, taking him as deep as I could without choking. I'm no expert at this so he wasn't all the way down my throat, but he was in far enough in that he was surrounded by warm wet heat.

He shuddered, inadvertently moving over my tongue for moment. He quickly realized that movement was a good thing and began rubbing himself along my tongue, teaching himself to fuck my mouth. I joined in, bobbing my head gently over him for added friction.

Gluub remained watching us and keeping me tied, until the moment he leaned over himself to lap at my juice, his tongue brushing Khaw's.

I can't pinpoint how or why but that turned me on. So I wondered...

I sucked lightly at Khaw then pulled myself back from his length and offered my tongue to Gluub. I wondered if he wished to taste Khaw on my tongue. Several of his eyes zoned in on my tongue and he leaned and opened his mouth to mine.

Those beautiful lips of his enclosed over my tongue, his own lapping at mine. I lost myself for a moment by tilting my head and kissing him. My lips nipped at his, caressing and sliding alternately, my tongue teasing his and exploring his mouth. All six eyed went wide and then hooded as he attempted to repeat my same movements.

Yes... Kiss me you silken-lipped ocean Siren. Wrap me in your arms, pull me close and ravage my mouth.

One day, once he learned more, I would have that. For now we explored and learned together.

I pulled back and he followed until I turned my head and slowly licked Khaw again. Gluub looked between me and Khaw's stiffness. I licked Khaw once more, my eyes on Gluub. The aviarid moaned low as I circled his tip with my tongue before engulfing him for a moment. I popped him out of my mouth and licked my lips at Gluub, teasing him.

Clearly I was not the only one adept at sexual teasing, because Gluub leaned his face towards me, as if offering a kiss, and watched my expression as he inserted Khaw's tip into his mouth and sucked.

I'm pretty sure I had a mini orgasm seeing that. For sure I squirted enough to wet the bed, which Khaw noticed and he began to lick me again. The Octoceph opened his mouth, inserting Khaw's entire length then slowly drawing him out. Khaw gasped and made a short peeping sound. Gluub looked... amused.

I leaned in and licked Khaw again, and this time Gluub joined me. Our tongues brushed each other as we went back and forth over Khaws stiffness which grew even larger and quaked lightly when we licked him together.

In the middle of this Khaw found that when he licked around my clitoris, I also quaked, and made more wetness. It was turning into his favorite game —

seeing how much wetness he could encourage from me then lapping it up.

That game came to its pinnacle when his tongue circled my clit at the same time Gluub figured out he could suck on Khaw when he was in his mouth. Khaw gasped and crowed softly, thrusting himself against Gluub's tongue, brushing over just the right spot on me, a tentacle tweaked my nipple as I watched this all happening, and threw my head back and spewed like a volcano.

Gluub joined Khaw in lapping at my cum as I lay there shuddering out the remains of my orgasm. One down, two to go.

I spread my legs more, tugging at the tentacles binding them and bringing both of their attention to me.

"I need my hands and feet." I wiggled my fingers. Gluub's limbs loosened and I immediately turned to grasp Khaw's stem, stroking him. When he started to press himself into my hand more, I motioned for him to come between my legs. The octoceph moved, making room for him. I continued stroking him for another few seconds then pulled him on top of me. He visibly melted as he stared into my eye, leaning forward to nuzzle my face and kiss me. It wasn't until I parked his tip at my entrance and used a heel to nudge him forward that he startled in surprise, eyes wide as saucers. Gluub brought his face right to where we were joined, watching both the process and each of our reactions at the same time, two eyes on each.

Khaw pushed further in and I winced slightly at the feeling of being so full. He immediately fretted, ruffling his feathers and making an upset sound. I instructed him to pull back then to come forward again but just a bit. Once again back, once again forward, until he slid inside me to his hilt.

The thick twists of the skin around him could be felt brushing over my insides once he was in me. I rested my hands on his hips and moved him back only a couple of inches then forward again a few times until his instincts crept in and he found himself moving back and forth inside me for friction.

He thrust into me as my ankles met the back of his thighs, encouraging him. He kissed me soundly, leaving his lips on mine as he worked himself into a frenzy at the spot where we met. It was actually sweet. Gluub was eyeing us intently and I noticed a parting between his layers of limbs. From there I watched a section of thinner smaller tentacles usher forth and tangle themselves together into a protrusion.

Was this how he mated? Or was he mimicking Khaw's cock so that he can join us?

Khaw's legs began to tremble as the pouch at the base of his cock began to fill, locking him into me. I felt the swelling though I think he remained unaware of the knot that began. He picked up speed with shorter thrusts, a low warble forming in his chest until he let out a squawk, spraying my insides and resting on top of me. That was when he noticed he was 'stuck' in me and became worried. I calmed him, stroking a hand over his back and having him rest until it began to release. Gluub faithfully watched every movement and every angle, learning.

When Khaw finished, I wondered how to suggest to Gluub that he come to me but he did not need any prompting. Strong tentacles eased Khaw to the side and Gluub rested between my legs. With a single move, he lifted me and carefully flipped me over then pulled me up onto my knees.

He really did learn a lot today, didn't he? I may need to send Maria something as thanks.

From behind, a tentacle wrapped around my throat, securing me. Another one grabbed a clump of my hair, manhandling me into a more preferred position — head to the side. Tentacles secured my thighs, opening me to his view.

I began to get a bit nervous, which he either scented or sensed because soothing petting motions smoothed down my back.

My lower parts were prodded open and exposed, tentacle tips rubbing up and down, spreading leftover wetness. I had no idea that Gluub's longer tentacles had hooks and sucker rings. Or that the suckers had tiny soft teeth attached. But I sure as hell know now, since he used them to part my lower lips at the center and spread me wider. I could feel the tugging but there was no pain. Tentacles pressed along me, filling and then leaving as he tested my inner width.

The grip on my hair tightened and I felt his weight on my back as a foreign presence began to invade me. The protrusion of tentacles he created writhed and moved as they stretched into me. I felt stray smaller fingerlings stroke over my clitoris as the mass grew and swell in my confines. If I was not aware of what was inside of me, I would have panicked and screamed. Even so, I was taken by surprise at the feeling of things moving inside of me as they entered and exited.

The fingerlings brushed wetness along my most sensitive parts while the wriggling intrusion thrust farther into me, causing me to gasp. He was thick at his base, though tapered, and not seeing or having any control lead to a hitch of fear in me.

He began to move back and forth, his slides in and out becoming jerky movements as he pinned me. I was still stretched wide open for his view and I gasped when a tentacle lashed at my bottom.

Did he just spank me?

He leaned forward and his lips kissed along my back, a loving contrast to the bondage and spanking.

His movements became fervorous and the parts spreading me open released. Suddenly it was just him leaning over me from behind, nuzzling my face as he pummeled my hole. Tentacles once again tweaked at my nipples and my breath caught at the twinge of pleasure.

Gluub moved to slamming himself into me, his flesh thwacking against mine each time as he went faster. He was ramming me so hard I had to brace from my head hitting the wall.

And then suddenly there was convulsing and whipping around in my core, and he wrapped himself around me and laid me to my side. I was facing Khaw, who was watching us, and we all simply laid there quietly.

DAYZEE

After taking my findings and going up the chain of command, my request for the larger bungalow on the corner of our land was approved!

It borders the food area, closer to Gluub and Khaws tribes so that we can easily visit and stay at any of the locations without there being issues. Of course who is going to give any of us issues when they have to deal with the other two as well? I may not have sharp feathers or tentacles but I grew up in a crappy neighborhood and had four brothers, so you can try me and find out.

The UGP is also elated that my "friendship" with Khaw and Gluub has also encouraged other tribes not only to interact with them but to attempt to communicate with me.

Look at us, hanging out with the natives! Yes ma'am, we are moving up on this planet's popularity list. Who knows, maybe there is an invite to somewhere cool in there and I can show them new places.

There will also be a raise in my future. Good thing, too, since I'm going to need to get us a larger bed :)

Author's Note

Anthologies consist of short stories, so this is a shortened 'anthology version' of the original. The full version will be released upon completion of the anthology's term.

Thank you for reading :)

MORE FROM CASS

We hope you enjoyed ***Invaded*** by Cass Alex!

This was book #1 in the new Monster Mouthfuls series, set in the same universe as the eagerly anticipated Visits from the Intergalactic Matchmaker series!

HER HORNED ALIEN

Living on the streets of Terra is a hard life for Gin. The last thing she needs is some big blue jerk of an alien giving her attitude!

Yah, she probably shouldn't have hidden in his spacecraft then...

Cass Alex is a multi-faceted author, with projects ranging from rehoming centers for wayward demons (UF), hellhound shifter training academies (PNR), alien matchmaking yentas (SFR), fun rom-coms and enemies-to-lovers standalones (ROM), mouthfuls of monster love madness (SFR-MON), an academy for oddballs (YA), a witch and the demon who randomly moved in (UF), paranormal safe cities (PNR), were's in space (SF/SFR), Area 52 (SCI-FI) and even more, all coming up! :)

WWW.CASSALEX.COM

AFTERWORD

Thank you for reading *Monsters After Dark!*

If we have awakened your enthusiasm for raunchy monster romance with 'uniquely' equipped heroes, you should definitely join the Facebook Readers' Group:

MONSTERS, DEMONS, AND KNOTTING, OH MY!
https://www.facebook.com/groups/monstersdemonsohmy

(It's exactly what it says on the tin)

Printed in Great Britain
by Amazon

70429943R00200